LOVE IS A NEW WORLD

When Elizabeth Carleton met Jake Bartlett, Rolfe Sumner's farm-hand, her life changed forever. Despite her thinking him handsome, he was still a hired man. But in sleepy Washington, Vermont, Elizabeth found herself loving him, agreeing to marry him and becoming the owner of Sumner farm. And when she discovered Jake's dark secret, she fought to win him back from the edge of habitual bleakness — and won. For Liz, the summer she met Jake was the summer that changed her forever.

Sharp, Helen

Love is a new
world / Helen
Sharp

LP

1735751

HELEN SHARP

LOVE IS A NEW WORLD

Complete and Unabridged

LINFORD
Leicester

First published in Great Britain in 1973 by
Robert Hale Limited
London

First Linford Edition
published 2006
by arrangement with
Robert Hale Limited
London

British Library CIP Data

Sharp, Helen, 1916 –
Love is a new world.—Large print ed.—
Linford romance library
1. Love stories
2. Large type books
I. Title
813.5'4 [F]

ISBN 1–84617–412–0

Published by
F. A. Thorpe (Publishing)
Anstey, Leicestershire

Set by Words & Graphics Ltd.
Anstey, Leicestershire
Printed and bound in Great Britain by
T. J. International Ltd., Padstow, Cornwall

This book is printed on acid-free paper

1

Growing-Up

New England in springtime is like a girl becoming a woman; it is demanding, it is frantic and teary, it is despairing and imperious, iron-hard and silk-soft. It yields, and it will not give an inch. It loves and hates, laughs and cries all at the same time.

It is beautiful, painfully so, and it is sad to see with slow dusk falling. In most ways it was the same way Elizabeth Carleton felt and looked and acted right up until her eighteenth birthday, but afterwards New England remained the same when Liz Carleton changed subtly and steadily into what she would be the rest of her life — a woman with all the needs and hungers, the desires and hopes and prayers that meant.

No one was happier when Liz Carleton's disposition settled into habit and conscience than her grandfather, Jasper Carleton, who had raised Liz since she'd been eleven when his son and his daughter-in-law were killed in an aeroplane accident on the outskirts of New York City on their one and only trip to Florida. It was on the way back that they were killed, along with seventy-seven other passengers.

Jasper Carleton had been a widower fifteen years when he went to get Liz and lead her down to his home in Washington, Vermont. The town was actually a village, and everyone who saw Liz walking from the north end to the south end with her grandfather, understood. There weren't very many dry eyes. But that had been seven or eight years earlier, and since that time, although Jasper had dug in and fought hard, and at times had seemed to be winning, it had been no easy thing, raising a leggy, coltish girl, because Jasper'd only had one child and it had been a son. All he knew about young girls he got out of a book the local librarian, Agatha Thorpe, had sent him, plus a little help from Agatha herself once in a while, when the stress got to be just a mite more than Jasper could cope with.

But Liz was on her way to being nineteen years old now, and, thanks be to the Lord, she had changed a great lot this past year. A very great lot, and it was truly a vast relief, because between her thirteenth year and her eighteenth birthday she was a pure trial to Jasper; so bad in fact he almost asked Mrs Thorpe to marry him in Liz's fourteenth year. Mrs Thorpe, the librarian, was a widow-woman who had raised three handsome daughters, all married now and moved away, all with babies of their own. She'd had her eye on Jasper Carleton for a number of years, and while he'd known and liked her most of his life — she was a wee bit younger than he was — after the passing of his wife of thirty-four years he just couldn't

3

bring himself to have another woman in that house south of town where he had lived all his married life. Seemed downright sacrilegious, he told her one time, and she'd never mentioned marriage again, except in Liz's fourteenth year when poor Jasper was fair out of his mind worrying.

'You could raise a barnful of boys to one girl,' Jasper used to say, and give off with an enormous sigh to emphasise it. 'I've got a world of respect for folks that raise girls. Imagine! Aggie Thorpe raised *three* after her husband died, and every blessed one turned out perfectly. A real credit to Aggie. I'm tempted to learn her secret, I truly am, but I'll try hanging on a mite longer.'

After Elizabeth's fourteenth year the change in her was more teary-eyed and tantrum-like than ever, but with a difference. She had spells when she was the sweetest, as well as promising to be the prettiest, girl in town. She would gather blueberries and bake a pie. She would bring her grandfather a dipperful

4

of cold water straight from the spring-house when he was out working in the garden, and in the evenings she would sit, lady-like, and listen while Jasper reminisced. He liked having someone to talk to, especially if they didn't interrupt.

But the very next day she might blame him because her hemline was crooked or because some boy at school told her she'd be pretty except for the freckles across the saddle of her nose.

At fifteen it was a little better, fewer tantrums and more giggly, and everlasting, conversations on the party-line, until Everette De Pugh, the telephone company's local manager, called Jasper to account about young girls tying up the line hour after hour. Then came sixteen and a few dates, less giggling, more soft, far-away looks, and gradually sixteen faded into seventeen and then eighteen. Jasper never did learn Aggie Thorpe's secret for raising young girls, but one day after a band concert around the Civil War cannon on the green when Aggie sighed and told him Liz was the prettiest girl in the whole county, he was perfectly satisfied that it had all been worth it.

'Looks like her mother,' he said, and Aggie nodded — then sniffled and said a fly had got in her eye.

Winter left, spring came, spring left and summer came. The fields ripened, brawny farm lads worked days and ran the town nights, folks sat on their front porches rocking and listening to the cicadas making their racket and the crickets too, in the mulched flower beds.

Washington, Vermont, named for a Virginian, was a village where change hung fire. The little valley where the town sat was apart, and it had no industry and very little commerce. Folks had been farming the same irregular little free-fenced fields for upwards of three hundred years, many in the same family. Not many visitors passed through, fewer holidaymakers because the nearest lake was seven miles back in the mountains by footpath, and there was neither an arterial carriageway nor a railroad. In the words of Everette De Pugh, a Massachusetts transplant, Washington, Vermont, had been dead for two hundred years and no one had had as yet the decency to bury it.

Jasper's response to that had been, 'When you want a fool to bray, go and get you a Massachusetts man.'

But the town did not grow, and that, or so the social planners said, was a sure-fire sign of retrogression and ultimate moribundity. Washington did not know it was supposed to turn moribund, so it just went on, day after day, year after year, reading in the newspapers and hearing on the television newscasts about a war here, an assassination there, a mass-murder somewhere else, without really being a part of the present at all, because the last murder committed in Washington had been back in 1876, the year Custer was wiped out by the redskins Out

West, when someone shot and killed the postman, stole the mail pouches, and to this day neither the pouches, the mail, nor the murderer, had ever turned up.

It was always assumed, though, that a known army deserter named Coon who had been hiding in the mountains for about ten years, and who was never seen again after the murder and robbery, had been the culprit.

The postman, John Hardesty, had been buried with all honours including a three-round blank-cartridge salute over the grave that made someone's cow hold up her milk for a week afterwards from purest fright, and had been sunk into his grave in his old war-time Union-blue cavalryman's uniform.

Jasper told about the cow. It had been his parents' animal, and his mother was mad as hops until Old Bossy started 'giving down' again, the last of old Hardesty's mourners.

There was one exception to the no-visitors rule; each summer the farmers hired field-help, and since most of the local lads were spoken for early, and there were never enough of them anyway, some farmers wrote their relations elsewhere in New England, and a trickle of outsiders came into town to harvest and hay and fallow the fields, and do whatever else was needed, like going back into the mountains to 'make' wood, as it was called, meaning felling and bucking up trees for winter stoves and furnaces.

Usually, these young men were either seniors in highschool, or were from some local college or University in their home state. Now and then a professional farmhand would walk in, but that was unusual. If a man really wanted to make a career out of being a farmhand, he could make a lot better wages in a place like Nebraska where the farms were many times larger than they were in Vermont, in most of New England, in fact. Also, the growing season in Vermont was short, the winters were severe, and it was a long while between haying-time and haying-time.

But the summer Elizabeth turned nineteen one of those professional farmhands arrived in the county, to work for old Rolfe Sumner, a yeasty bachelor of bitter vintage who was reputedly the richest farmer, and biggest miser, in all Vermont. He might have been the former, but almost any town in the State could have put up its own aspirant for that second record; it was common knowledge that in the entire United States New Englanders were the most abstemious, the most cantankerous, and the most hoardingest. The last New England President worthy of the name, Calvin Coolidge, had been so miserly he hadn't even liked to use his vocabulary unless whatever he'd had to say could be grunted out in less than a dozen words.

Rolfe Sumner was a bleak, rawboned old man, presumably in his seventies. Jasper Carleton said he *had* to be in his seventies, because Jasper went to school with him, and went off to World War One with him, and Jasper made no secret of his age; he was sixty-nine the previous spring. 'Rolfe Sumner was three grades ahead of me in school. He was growing a beard when my voice changed, so he's got to be into his seventies. But it'd do no good to ask the old skinflint; he'd charge a man just for giving him the time of day.'

Rolfe Sumner's professional farm-hand was also rawboned, lanky and spare, but he looked to be no more than perhaps twenty-three or twenty-four, and he was a quiet, tanned, taffy-haired, blue-eyed man with worlds of endurance. Even old Rolfe, who would have allowed wild horses to pull him to pieces before he'd have paid a compliment, said in the tavern one evening over a chilled beer that he had never in all his born days seen a man like Jake Bartlett, his hired-hand. 'That man never tires. I've set him at jobs just to see if he wouldn't give out. He don't.'

'Paces himself,' opined another farmer, down the bar a few seats. 'I know the kind. But they aren't them schoolboys, I can tell you. In fact, except in a professional, you don't see that breed much any more.'

'Like sinew and steel,' said old Rolfe, peering into his glass; beer was a dime more expensive nowadays than it had been when Rolfe had been in his drinking prime, it behoved a man to cherish it a mite. 'But he's not a New Englander. Didn't say where he was from when I hired him on. Just said, 'Mister Sumner, if you want a worker, I'll hire on. But if you want someone to stand around here all morning answering questions, reckon I'll just move on to the next farm.' Short with me, like that, and I was of half a mind to send him down the road.'

'Why didn't you?' asked someone across the room.

Rolfe sipped beer, then said, 'I've been hiring them, man and boy, for over half a century. I know the way they look, them as will work hard. Jake Bartlett's the best hired-hand I've had in all them years. Absolutely the best.'

2

The Crisis

In Washington, Vermont, each year there was some kind of crisis. It never had much to do with national crises, and certainly not international crises, but it gave folks something to talk about, like the dairyman west of town who owned three cows and each had one set of twins, the year Liz turned eighteen. Very unusual to get one set, but *three* sets the same year in the same herd was almost unheard of.

But the summer of Elizabeth's nineteenth birthday the year was half gone and nothing had happened. The winter before a blizzard had knocked out the power lines for twelve hours, but that hardly qualified as a crisis in Vermont, where every winter the electricity was out for at least that long.

Otherwise, there had been nothing happen, except the Presidential election, and Washington, Vermont, turned out to cast its solidly Conservative vote as it had always done, but that wasn't a crisis, either.

The village had no doctor, couldn't support one, but there was a Registered Nurse, Mrs Eulalia Wilson, a widow with liquid dark eyes and a downy moustache who folks thought was Italian or Spanish, or maybe one of those black French-Canadians, while in fact she was a Puerto Rican who had come to Washington when her husband, a career navy man, had retired. He had been born in Washington. Also, he died there, six years after his retirement, and Mrs Wilson never departed. It was difficult to understand why not; she was a Latin of some kind and Vermont winters couldn't be a Latin's idea of pleasure. But whatever her reason, Eulalia Wilson stayed on, delivering an occasional baby, doctoring the aged, scolding the accidentally injured, and in general ruling the town without one bit of competition from the medical standpoint.

Eulalia used to walk down of a summer evening and sit with Jasper and Elizabeth on the porch of the old Carleton house. It was her opinion that no one in the entire county could make wild blackberry wine as well as Jasper Carleton.

Elizabeth liked Eulalia very much; she did not possess a single New England inhibition: whatever Eulalia Wilson thought, she said. Eulalia had also been Elizabeth's confidante during the troublesome years. When Jasper ran to Aggie Thorpe, Elizabeth had gone discreetly to Eulalia's house over on Lincoln Avenue. They had sat in the kitchen in wintertime, close to the roaring woodstove, talking woman-to-woman.

Elizabeth was one of the few people in the village who knew where Puerto Rico was, and Eulalia Wilson was one of the few people in Washington,

Vermont, who knew what being an orphan was; she had also been one, many years ago.

If there was a crisis in town, Eulalia Wilson was ordinarily in the thick of it. If there was a feud starting or a fight going, she was usually involved in those things too. Eulalia was a self-appointed constable as well as a Registered Nurse. She was vocal, opinionated, compassionate to a fault, and absolutely convinced she knew right from wrong.

The day old Rolfe Sumner drove in from the farm to see her, to sit and drink tea with her and talk of everything under the sun except what had brought him, Elizabeth was there, at her house, but she left shortly after Rolfe arrived, which seemed to ease the old man's mind a little, but not until Eulalia had watched him drink three cups of tea, growing steadily more impatient with each cup, did she demand to know why he had come.

'Standing in the doorway of my barn,' he said, mumbling his words as though reluctant to make some admission. 'Just standing there, Eulalia, when all at once I was as breathless as though I'd run a mile.'

Eulalia's black eyes flashed. 'When did this happen?'

'Well, what time is it now? It happened maybe two hours ago.'

'Has it ever happened before?'

'No.'

'And right now, this minute, do you feel tired; maybe you have a slight aching in the arms, in the joints all the way down to the wrists?'

Rolfe lifted hard old faded blue eyes to Eulalia's face. 'You've figured it. Now tell me what it is.'

Eulalia faltered. 'How old are you, Rolfe?'

'Old enough. What's that got to do with it?'

The warm, dark eyes flashed sudden, black lightning. 'You answer my questions, Rolfe Sumner, or go get someone else to look after you. Would you like another cup of tea?'

'No, ma'm. I mean, no thank you, and I'm seventy-four years old.'

Eulalia sat and considered the old man with the seamed, weathered face. 'You have a good hired man?'

'The best.'

'Rolfe,' said Eulalia, speaking softly but intently, 'seventy-four is a respectable age. Do you understand that? Let your hired man do the work. You have earned the right to lie abed longer each morning and to sit on the porch during the heat of these summertime days. Do you have a demanding family? No. Then what is the point in trying to kill yourself working?'

'But I wasn't working,' he responded, 'and that is the point. I was standing there in the shade of the barn. Eulalia, what was it, my lungs?'

She smiled and leaned impulsively to pat his work-enlarged hands. 'Rolfe, it was your heart, and it was signalling to you that the time has come to stop working.'

He seemed to hear only the last two

words. 'I can't stop working.'

Eulalia turned and pointed out the window across the roadway where Washington's time-hallowed cemetery stood, shaded by giant birches and beeches. 'Yes you can. If you don't Rolfe, Someone Else will see to it that you stop.'

The old man slumped slowly, and when Eulalia looked back again, he was different. She knew the symptoms. 'You are not beaten. Life can never beat a strong man. You can live a long while yet, and be active as well, but no more of the back-breaking *hard* work, Rolfe.' She smiled. 'You should be pleased. Now you can drive into town and sit with your friends at the green.'

He snorted derisively. 'Those old has-beens!'

Eulalia did not push it. 'I'll get you more tea. Sit still.'

He probably wouldn't have moved if the roof had collapsed. In seventy-four years he had never had to face anything like this; he was strong, he was comfortably well-off, and until this day he had seemed practically immortal. Now, suddenly, he was not only *not* immortal, he was on the sundown side of life. It was a terrible blow, being both fallible and vulnerable the same day.

Eulalia returned with the pot and refilled both their teacups. She pinched lemon into his tea and put sugar in hers; she seemed hardly to see the change her words had wrought as she resumed her chair in the warm parlour and said, 'There just is no simple way to tell a person, Rolfe, when the time arrives for them to slow down, to slacken off, as you say in Vermont. But you know as well as I do that it happens to all of us eventually. Look, twenty years ago I danced all night and drove with my husband two hundred miles to a fiesta, and back again, without sleeping. Well, now it would kill me.' She laughed. 'Drink your tea.'

He drank it, obediently, like a child, but he left shortly afterwards all dammed up inside himself, and when

Eulalia saw Elizabeth in Brown's market the next day, she told Liz something that was on her mind the balance of the day after Rolfe Sumner had been to see her.

'Everything changes a personality, Elizabeth. Did you know that? Say an angry word to someone and their personality is made to cower a little. The process is endless. Yesterday I told old Rolfe Sumner he'd had a heart tremor, and you'd have thought I'd told him to go quickly and make his will. You will notice the change.'

Elizabeth *might* notice the change, but not very soon because, although she knew Mister Sumner well, their paths had no occasion to cross very often. In fact, before she saw Rolfe Sumner again — at the time when he was providing the village with its annual crisis — she had all but forgotten what Eulalia Wilson had told her.

The way she happened to see Rolfe Sumner at his crucial moment was slightly odd, too; she was not a very punctual church- or civic-minded person when it came time to get out and sell chances on the Independence Day turkey raffle, but this year she co-operated because the Chairman of the Chamber of Commerce himself, Jonathon Brown, who owned the general store, nailed her at his meat counter and talked her into making the rounds.

Every year the raffle was supposed to be bigger than it had been the year before, and every year it was pretty much the same; after all, there were just so many people, the same ones, who attended every summer, give or take maybe two dozen.

Nonetheless, Elizabeth fired up her grandfather's old car and started making her rural rounds. Everyone bought at least one ticket, even those people who were donating the turkeys. It was customary, Just like it was customary for everyone to come into town and watch the parade of war veterans, listen to the band play stirring

22

marches on the green, and watch Jasper Carleton, the only one who dared, fire the Civil War cannon in celebration of Independence Day. When Liz drove into the Sumner farmyard, three miles north of town, she had no reason under the sun to consider it possible that anything out of the ordinary might occur; she expected to sell two tickets, one to Rolfe Sumner, one to his hired man, and be on her way to the next farm. But this day she never got one step farther.

When she alighted from the car out front of the old house, there was a strange, deep silence to the yard, and a tractor stood over near the equipment shed, motor idling, but it was near noontime, so the menfolk could be inside eating.

She started through the sagging old picket gate towards the front porch before the feeling came over her that everything was not right. Still, she went to the door and knocked. Inside, the sound bounced from wall to wall and earned her no response, so she knocked again, harder this time, and from beyond the gloomy open door of the equipment shed across the farmyard a man's voice sang out.

'Come over here. Come over here, and hurry!'

She did not question the command because there had been an unmistakable urgency in the voice, so she went back out through the gate and walked briskly over, past the idling tractor, to the shady, cool opening of the equipment shed. There, the sight she saw stopped her cold.

A sweat-stained young man with tousled taffy hair was down on one knee upon the cobblestone floor of the shop, holding something that hissed to the face of old Rolfe Sumner, who was limp at the younger man's feet. When Elizabeth halted, a hand flying to her mouth, the young man looked up and said, 'Lady, come over here. Do you see this green handle I'm trying to turn on the oxy tank of the acetylene welder?

Well, when I tell you to turn it, do so, but turn it very slightly and very gently. Lady! Don't stand there! Do as I say!'

The last few words were fired at her like bullets, jarring her from her stunned sensation. She went ahead and reached for the nicked old green handle to the oxygen tank of the welding cradle. At once the lanky young man loosened his hold and was able to employ both hands holding the cupped mask of red bandana handkerchief over old Rolfe's face better. 'Oxygen!' he snapped. 'Slow now, lady, and easy. Keep your mind on what you're doing!'

She turned the little handle ever so slightly and a hissing sound ensued. She was watching the grey, lifeless face under the young man's hands. 'He looks dead,' she murmured.

The young man didn't comment about that; he was bending low, evidently trying to see whether Rolfe was ingesting the pure oxygen. Finally, he leaned back. 'A little more, lady, and remember what I told you — slow and gentle.'

She obeyed. 'What happened?'

'He got off the tractor and walked over here where I was welding new ploughshares. He started to wobble. I saw him put a hand to his shirtfront and squeeze the cloth, then he started down and I ran and caught him. My guess, lady, is that he had a heart attack.' The young man looked up at Liz. 'I'm Jake Bartlett, I work for Mister Sumner as his farmhand.' He smiled slightly.

She said, 'I'm Elizabeth Carleton . . . I came by to sell him — and you — some chances on the Fourth of July turkey raffle.' It sounded so inane she almost didn't finish it. Jake Bartlett did not seem to notice; he was bending low again, looking for some kind of flutter or gasp, or maybe a twitching muscle.

Liz said, 'Is he — alive, Mister Bartlett?'

'Another quarter-turn on the oxygen handle,' he said, ignoring the question.

'I don't suppose Washington has an ambulance, perhaps with an oxygen tank and mask in it?'

'Nothing like that,' she conceded.

He straightened up. 'He's taking it. His eyelids moved. Well, we'll keep him coming on as long as we can, then you'd better beat it down to the village and get someone to come back up here with a light truck of some kind so we can lay him out on the rack and take this tank of oxygen right along with him.'

Liz nodded. It all sounded very logical. She finally switched her attention from old Rolfe to his hired man. Jake Bartlett didn't act nor talk quite like the run-of-the-mill farmhands, and that both piqued her and troubled her.

3

The Farmhand

Eulalia Wilson took over the moment they delivered Rolfe Sumner to her house, where three back bedrooms had been fitted to accommodate patients, the nearest the village had to a hospital. She would even have lent a hand at getting him indoors if Jake Bartlett hadn't picked Rolfe up like a baby and carried him effortlessly to the bed that Eulalia had prepared for him.

And later, when Liz and Jake were in the parlour, along with Everette De Pugh of the telephone company's local office, who had furnished the flatbed truck to bring Rolfe to town, and Eulalia had a moment to do so, she came forward to thank them all for their co-operation, for their help, and sent both De Pugh and Elizabeth away, asking young Bartlett to remain because someone had to help her devise a way to make that oxygen tank functional in the sick-room.

This was the first time Eulalia met Jake Bartlett, too. She usually got to know some of the farmhands who came and went; they were either more accident-prone than other people, or their work resulted in more bodily injuries; in either event, she got to know them, but Jake had never been to see her.

He surprised Eulalia. When they were devising ways to use the oxygen tank, he demonstrated a detailed knowledge of oxygen masks ordinary people did not possess. She said something about that, too, but Jake simply smiled and went on with his work.

Rolfe was resting. He looked and seemed completely exhausted. Eulalia said it was a miracle that he was not dead. She also had something to say about his not taking her advice, but Jake corrected that on the spot.

'He took your advice, he told me about the tremor and what you had told him. He was demoralised, but he was not so foolish as to believe he didn't have to ease off.'

'Wasn't he driving a tractor?' asked Eulalia, who had this from Liz.

'Yes, but driving a tractor through an apple orchard is no more strenuous than driving a car through the village on Saturday night. Take my word for it, Mrs Wilson, he was easing off. But — after this, I guess easing off isn't going to be enough, is it?'

Eulalia cocked her head and watched the capable large hands of Jake Bartlett fashion a very efficient cone for the oxygen application. She ignored his question in favour of one of her own. 'You have not always been a farmhand, have you, Mister Bartlett? Maybe, in the army you were a medical aidman?'

He laughed down into her tilted face. 'Very good. That's exactly what I was in the army. Three years of it, under some pretty darned adverse conditions.'

'But they need men like you in the big city hospitals,' exclaimed Eulalia.

His nice smile lingered. 'No. No big city, not even a big city hospital. No one needs me, but me.' He offered her the improvised oxygen cone. 'Care to try it?'

She didn't; there was no immediate need because Rolfe was somewhere between consciousness and unconsciousness, breathing evenly. 'He should be dead,' she said, leaning to look at the patient and to feel for his pulse. 'But for you, he would be.'

Bartlett placed the oxygen cone atop the tank, wiped smudges off the gauge that told how much oxygen was still in the tank, and leaned loosely upon the wall, studying the grey old face on the pillow. 'I suppose it's fair to wonder if you are doing them any favour, or not,' he said, softly. 'What's ahead for him? He had been active all his life. Now — now, he's half-man, half-vegetable. Some big favour I did him.'

'He will be much better,' said Eulalia,

raising up from using a stethoscope. 'It wasn't one of the massive ones. Rolfe Sumner is a very fortunate old man, but he *is* an old man, and, like it or not, he's going to have to recognise that.' She kept her dark eyes on the tanned, handsomely rugged face across the bed from her. 'He won't be half-vegetable unless he wills it.'

Bartlett kept smiling, but his blue eyes were dark with poignancy. 'Like caging an old eagle, Mrs Wilson. Which is the better way : a strenuous and fatal blaze of glory, or a slow, slow wasting away?'

'Neither, Mister Bartlett. For a man no older than you seem to be, you have a battered spirit.'

He laughed and straightened up off the wall. 'Well, I don't think you need me any longer, do you?'

She didn't, so he departed, and until she walked back out front it did not occur to her that he had ridden in with old Rolfe and had no car of his own to cover the three miles back to the farm in. She was annoyed with herself for having overlooked that, while on the other hand, although she had a car, she could not have left Rolfe Sumner alone long enough to drive his farmhand back to the Sumner place.

Well, it was a beautiful afternoon for hiking. A bit warm, perhaps, but clear and summer-sweet.

Liz returned in the evening and Eulalia told her of the oversight. She also said Rolfe was resting very well, better in fact than he had any right to rest because, massive or not, this time the tremor was very serious.

'Mister Bartlett saved his life, there is no doubt of that. You and Mister Bartlett together, Liz; his quick wittedness with that oxygen made the difference. Did you know he was once a corpsman in the army, a medical aidman?'

Liz knew nothing at all about Jake Bartlett except that he gave orders like someone who expected to be obeyed. She told Eulalia how it had been out at the equipment shed and the older woman was interested. She said Jake Bartlett was more than a farmhand, and that piqued both their curiosities. But later, when Eulalia could, she asked Rolfe, and all he knew about his hired man was that he did not answer questions very readily.

As for Rolfe, he had provided the community with its crisis. Folks would relate his heart-seizure with things for a long time to come; for example, when the Fourth of July celebration was held, it was afterwards referred to as the year of the celebration that came shortly after Rolfe Sumner's heart attack.

Rolfe did not get to participate. He was still bedridden when the shindig came off out at the edge of town on the village green, although he could, and did, get up now and then and make weak progress through Eulalia's house, sometimes to the rear garden where he could sit in sunshine and listen to Jake tell him about things at the farm. He was doing that dressed in the robe

Elizabeth Carleton had brought him as a present, when the Independence celebration opened with the National Anthem. He told Jake it was the first time he'd missed one of those things since he'd been a small boy.

Jake understood. 'You're entitled to miss one. Next year you'll be there to make up for this year.'

'Confounded good chance this time next year I'll be in the apple orchard,' said the old man. 'Jake, it's asking more of a hired hand than's right to ask, but that's where I'd like to be planted when the times comes, and seeing that I've got no kin, could I lay this obligation on you?'

Jake nodded without saying something reassuring. They were men together, thinking the kind of honest thoughts men faced without saying pointless things. Neither of them was a child in need of reassurance; people lived, and they died.

Rolfe smiled. 'Well, you'd better get over there and see if you won a turkey.'

Jake agreed, neglecting to mention he did not have a ticket. Somehow, in all the upset lately, when he had been thrown against Elizabeth Carleton, the subject of the turkey raffle never came up again, after that day in the equipment shed.

Jake did not own a car, but he had the use of Rolfe's vehicle, so after he left Eulalia's place he drove over to the green, had to go a considerable distance to find a place to park, then he walked back with the beech and chestnut and aspen trees making pleasant shadows all along the way. Odd thing about a windblown leaf, it settled to earth where something it knew not, said this is the place. Jake had fallen in love with Washington the first day. He still thought of it as something unreal, out of step with the world, but wonderfully uncomplicated and serene. Maybe the natives knew what they had and maybe they didn't, but *Jake* knew.

The lilting voice came from a small group of people. 'How is the patient,

Mister Bartlett?'

He turned, smiling as he searched her out. 'I just left him. He's looking much better.'

Elizabeth introduced him to her grandfather, to the De Pughs, all four of them, and to Jonathon Brown who was this year's Independence Day's co-ordinator. He was perspiring profusely and seemed to be the least relaxed man on the green.

The De Pughs drifted away. Jasper was taken in tow by Jonathon, and that left Elizabeth with Jake Bartlett. He said, 'In thinking back, I owe you an apology. I was darned brusque out there at the equipment shed that day.'

She shook her head at him. 'You did exactly the right thing. You were rather heroic, actually. And I hardly noticed the other thing.' She looked at him, thinking of the things Eulalia had said, and it *did* seem odd that he was here, in Vermont, as a farmhand, a labourer. She had no illusion about him being a prince in disguise, a millionaire seeking peace, anything like that, but she *did* feel interest.

He watched the uniformed bandsmen, mostly close to middle age, form up over by the Civil War cannon, and smiled. 'It's like 1920,' he said, and looked round at her. 'Where else in America today do they still celebrate Independence Day like this?'

She knew what he meant, but she said, 'Lots of places. In New Hampshire, over in Massachusetts. We're not all that old-fashioned.'

He cocked an eye at her. 'I didn't mean it like that. And I think it's great. But . . . well, let's just forget it.'

She smiled. She had no desire to inhibit him, and he seemed easily inhibited; he seemed, in fact, to be very sensitive. She remembered what Eulalia had said about destroying or at least altering personalities. She had no wish to do anything like that to him.

She reversed herself. 'You're right, of course. It's out of step with current scepticism and cynicism. But then, aren't we all a little unreal, here in Washington, Vermont?'

He studied her expression and her features. His eyes were clear and pleasant; he was one of those people who could smile very easily, evidently; it was always lurking, waiting for a chance to show, that smile of his.

'Sometimes I write bad poetry, usually about things like this. The new world with its separation of fact and fantasy. There they are, from a war that ended thirty years ago, ready to play the National Anthem without any real idea that they didn't beat anyone, thirty years ago, and they didn't wring any promises from anyone, because today we're in greater danger than ever, but there they are, full of a sense of honour because they did their duty.'

Elizabeth turned, compelled to do it by his words, and saw the volunteer band. She knew every face there, and most of them she liked. 'They did their duty,' she told him. 'I doubt that any of them expected to accomplish anything great. It's your and my generation that have ridiculed them because they didn't abolish suffering and win the world. Well, so far, Mister Bartlett, what has your and my generation done that is so wonderful, besides criticise?'

He laughed at her. 'I just keep touching nerves with you, don't I? But I'm not trying to do that. I'd sure like to think of you as a friend. I don't have very many here. As for the band — you are probably right; how many soldiers ever really know what they fight for?'

She said, 'Did you?'

He hesitated before answering. 'At the time, yes, but that turned out wrong, which is pretty darned disillusioning. No one wants to be wrong, but least of all when they are trying not to be killed at the same time.'

There was an ice-cream stand over beyond the band beneath some huge trees. He asked if she would like to have a dish of ice-cream with him. She was willing, but less because she wanted ice-cream than because her interest in him made her want to hear more of what he thought and felt.

They crossed the grass and went to the far side of the ice-cream booth, the side that wasn't very crowded, and ordered. That was when the band struck up, only it wasn't the National Anthem, it was a robust Sousa march, the kind that made people snap their fingers in time. She looked at him and smiled. They were both thinking the same thing about that kind of music; it really *did* belong to the 1920s.

There were a number of places where they could avoid the crowd and sit in tree shade to eat their ice-cream. He picked exactly the right spot, far enough back so that although a lot of people saw her sitting there with the tanned, brawny stranger, and would be certain to gossip about it next week, at least no one would come along to interfere.

He had a gentle manner and a delightful sense of humour. In fact, he was one of those unobtrusive individuals who grew on people. She was immensely curious, too, because he did not make the customary tell-tale grammatical errors of most rural people. In fact, she was perfectly willing to make a wager, by the time they'd finished their ice-cream, that he'd been to college and had graduated.

4

Dog Days

Rolfe's recovery was very slow, and as Eulalia told Jake one hot summer evening out on the front porch, when it was time for old Rolfe to leave her little private sanitorium the best thing he could do was move into a house he owned in the village and not go back to the farm, because the next attack was very likely going to be very serious, perhaps even fatal. She wondered if Jake could make Rolfe do that.

Jake didn't think so. 'Mrs Wilson, I'm only his farmhand. I've known him less than four months. Surely there are old friends here in the village that could talk and make him listen, better than I could.'

Eulalia didn't know. 'He believes in you very strongly, Jake. You are his only link with something he's known all his life, the farm. As time passes he gets to rely more and more on you.'

Bartlett left, looking a little troubled. Whether he implemented his discussion with Eulalia the next time he visited Rolfe or not, he never said, and it was almost impossible for Eulalia to get anything out of Rolfe he did not wish to talk about.

Liz came over one hot afternoon with some produce from her grandfather's garden. She and Rolfe Sumner sat out back in the shade of a huge old apple tree and talked away the better part of the afternoon. Rolfe reminisced about her grandfather and the First World War. She had heard it all before, but she was a good listener, and when the opening came she asked about Jake.

Rolfe gazed quietly at her. 'He told me nothing except that he doesn't like answering personal questions. Why? What difference does it make, Eliza-beth? A man can only be one of two things, worthwhile or worthless; all the rest of it is just so much detail.'

She smiled. 'He could have a wife and ten children somewhere, Mister Sumner, or he could have absconded with a suitcase full of money from a bank.'

Rolfe didn't see the difference. 'Then he'd be one of the worthless ones, is all.'

'Is he a good cook?' asked Liz, and Rolfe showed some surprise.

'A good cook? There's no such thing as the average man being a good cook.'

'Then maybe someone here in town should invite him to a decent meal now and again, Mister Sumner,' said Liz, and laughed at the expression the old man got across his bleached-out, weathered countenance. 'No, it's nothing like that. But he *was* heroic, and the least we can do is show some appreciation.'

'He'd be a fool not to accept,' opined old Rolfe, and after Elizabeth had departed and Eulalia came to herd him back indoors, he repeated that to her.

'Elizabeth Carleton wants that young man of mine to come to supper at her house. He'd have to be simple in the head not to accept. Why, when I was his age, if Elizabeth Carleton had asked me to jump, I'd simply have said, 'How high, ma'm?' '

Eulalia paused, distracted by this. 'They had ice-cream at the celebration together. But still and all, he is only a farmhand, eh?'

That stung old Rolfe so he turned and glowered. 'Only a farmhand? Let me tell you that some of the best men this country ever produced at one time or another were — only farmhands.'

Eulalia backed off quickly. 'I understand that. What I meant was — she is the most beautiful girl in Washington, maybe even in all Vermont, and what has he to offer?'

Rolfe didn't like this kind of talk any better. 'He's honest and hard-working, clean and upstanding. And he's the best worker I ever saw, and I've seen quite a few. Now then, I'd say those are traits to recommend him.'

Eulalia gave up. 'Jasper Carleton sent over a batch of vegetables from his garden. I thought that was very nice of him.'

Rolfe agreed, but in a tone of voice that made it clear he had not recovered from his indignation yet. When they were inside and Eulalia barred the back door, he turned and said, 'One reason I never had much to do with womenfolk: they demand too much from a man. They've put a lot of good ones into their grave.'

Eulalia came around very slowly, her black eyes brilliant with surprise and fury. 'Was that for my benefit?' she asked in a voice that had sunk so low it was barely audible.

Rolfe saw his mistake at once. And as a matter of fact he hadn't been thinking of Eulalia's late husband at all. He had had in mind just making a general statement.

He was thunderstruck by how this was turning out. So thunderstruck in fact that he swallowed twice before even attempting to dig his way out with words.

'Lordy sakes, no, Miz' Wilson. I wasn't thinking of anyone in particular, but you least of all. What I meant was that maybe some folks won't like the idea of my hired man seeing Elizabeth Carleton, but as far as I'm concerned he's good enough, because he's a decent, honest soul.'

Eulalia's fury diminished slowly. She pointed towards the hall, which meant for old Rolfe to go down and take his daily bath before supper. He turned and moved off without another word.

As far as Eulalia was concerned, it wasn't a matter of Jake Bartlett being good enough for Elizabeth Carleton, because Eulalia had not been thought good enough for her husband, many years ago, so she suffered from as little bigotry as anyone, but what Eulalia had in mind was Elizabeth's security. An itinerant farmhand was hardly likely to be able to look after a wife like

Elizabeth, and after a while it was easy to imagine the heartache, the disillusionment, the deep and silent regret. Eulalia had seen it happen.

But living the life of another person was impossible too, particularly when there was someone like Rolfe Sumner to look after, and lately Eulalia had had another patient or two, so, except for fixing it in her mind that Elizabeth shouldn't see too much of that handsome farmhand, Eulalia had neither the time nor the inclination to do anything else about it but worry, and she even had to do that sporadically.

Elizabeth didn't worry. Neither did Jasper, but then her grandfather hardly qualified; as far as he was concerned, when Liz wanted to use the old car to go get Mister Bartlett and bring him back for supper, it was perfectly agreeable with her grandfather. He'd already heard enough about Jake Bartlett to be interested. Moreover, it would be nice, just once, to see a man's face across the supper table.

Elizabeth drove out beyond town, the three miles to the Sumner place, about two in the afternoon. When she pulled into the yard there wasn't a soul in sight, and the place was as still as it had been that fateful day when she'd driven in before.

For a moment she had a fluttery heart, then she saw him, or his shadow, move across a soiled window in the equipment shed. Apparently he hadn't heard her drive up. She crossed to the cool doorway and he looked up from a workbench where he'd been about to weld two segments of a machine part, which were balanced upon bricks until he could make the initial tack.

He removed the welding helmet, put aside the unlighted torch, smiled and said, 'This seems to be our rendezvous point, and it's pretty grimy with the accumulation of a half-century of soot.'

She looked around. The old shop had tools for every imaginable job hanging from wall-spikes. There was an ancient forge and scar-faced anvil. Workbenches lined three walls, and soiled old cupboards stood above each one. This was probably the dirtiest segment of a man's world she had ever seen, but she could appreciate men enjoying themselves here.

He waited until she'd finished her assessment, then laughed. 'Grubby place, isn't it? But every farm needs one.' He pointed. 'You could even shoe horses here, if there were still horses on farms. Otherwise you can make major overhauls and repairs on tractors or pumps or any kind of machinery.' He paused, considered her, then said, 'Not another turkey raffle?'

'Dinner tonight at our house,' she told him. 'Bachelor cooking, they tell me, is one of the prime causes of ulcers.'

'Or ptomaine,' he averred. 'I'm very grateful. What time?'

'You can come back with me, and I'll drive you back afterwards.'

He demurred. 'It'll take me a half-hour just to scrub the grease off.

Why don't you go on ahead, and I'll drive Mister Sumner's car in?'

She was agreeable to that. 'The house is at the southern end of town.'

He surprised her. 'I know where it is. The Carleton place.'

She gazed at him, then decided against asking the obvious question. 'All right. In about an hour then?'

He nodded, left the bench and strolled back out across the summer-hot yard with her to her grandfather's car, out front of the house. As he opened the door for her he said, 'It's mighty nice of you folks to send garden produce over to Mrs Wilson's place. And that robe for Mister Sumner.' He closed the door and stood looking down at her. 'I wouldn't mind getting sick.'

'You can't. Who'd run the farm?'

'The crops are in; from now until harvest there's not too much to do. I'll make some wood, mend fences, do odds and ends, but I could make the time to be sick.' He grinned. 'See you in about an hour.' After she backed around and drove off, he leaned on the old fence looking out where dust-banners fell rearward as she went back towards town.

She was something very special. Not just in build, in looks, but in temperament and sweetness. She was one of those women men *feel* about even before they know them. It was a kind of strange *rapport*; he had walked into crowded hotel lobbies and airports, and felt the pull of some particular woman, had raised his head, looking around, and had seen her eyes lift to him too. There was no explaining it, but it was a power, a force, something magnetic that sliced through everything that separated one man from one particular woman.

Elizabeth Carleton affected him that way. If he did as much for her, she gave no sign of it. He turned to march slowly back to the shop and finish his welding. But she wouldn't ever let a man know anyway.

He worked at the shop for fifteen

minutes, then went over to his room off the rear of the old house to shower and clean up. It had been a hot day. Vermont, for all its bitter and long winters, was also capable of midsummer heat too, except that it was never a very dry kind of heat. The humidity remained moderately high. It was possible to hang a shirt on a chair-back at bedtime, for a short time in Vermont during the summer, and arise the next morning to find that it was still clammy. The humidity wasn't as bad as it was in the tropics, but it certainly was a lot higher than it was in the desert.

When Jake finished dressing, though, he felt much cooler, and if the sun would drop and dusk would come, he might even be able to make the drive down to the Carleton place without getting a limp collar all over again.

The trouble with that was that he didn't have the time to waste before the sun descended. It did not depart until very late this time of year. Eight or nine o'clock sometimes.

Outside, the heat was there but diminishing a little, grudgingly, a few degrees at a time, and although Rolfe Sumner's car was not old, it did not have air conditioning. In fact, Jake smiled to himself imagining the reaction if some enterprising car salesman had ever tried to sell Rolfe Sumner on air conditioning for a car.

Jake did not actually consider Rolfe miserly, but he knew the kind well enough to realise that they never spent a cent unless they had to. Where they got the reputation for being miserly was from their refusal, after seventy years of getting along very well without it, to part with a penny for something they considered frivolous — like air conditioning inside a car.

In a sense, the Rolfe Sumners of New England were correct, too. For no more than perhaps two months out of the whole year, an air-conditioned car would be pleasant. In exchange for that brief period of comfort, the cost was about a quarter as much as the entire car cost. Basically, that was how the Rolfe Sumners viewed such things, and they were right, of course, but on the drive down to the village through shimmering waves of gelatin-like late-day heat, Jake had to assert that this was so with more emphasis than at any other time of year.

His collar did go limp, too, before he reached town and cruised on through, heading for the southern environs. Fortunately, it was evening and would soon be dusk, then limp collars went mostly unnoticed, and it was also fortunate that around Washington, Vermont, sartorial pre-eminence, or even sartorial averageness, meant very little. Vermonters were a realistic bunch; they pretty much subscribed to the belief that men only came in two kinds, decent ones and poor-quality ones, and the finest clothes in the world couldn't change a man's outlook nor his black heart, if he had one.

5

The Guest for Dinner

For Elizabeth the dinner was average. Roast beef with fresh vegetables, a pineapple salad, and coffee. While she made the finishing touches Jake Bartlett went out back with her grandfather to look at the rather extensive garden Jasper planted every summer. There were some crops, such as early corn, that Jasper never had much success with, because the occasional early frosts caught them, but his hardier crops, beets, pumpkins, squashes, onions, and even potatoes, were thriving.

It was a very ambitious garden for a man Jasper's age, but he had never planted a smaller one. Jake's experienced eye appreciated the mulched beds, the lack of weeds, and the carefully engineered arterial through-ways for the irrigation water which, while not always needed because of summertime rains, nevertheless were there in case water was needed when the rains were not co-operative. 'Vermont is a lot like England,' explained old Jasper, who had been in Britain half a century earlier, during the First World War. 'We get enough moisture, generally speaking, never to have to worry much about irrigation, but some of my crops need more than just a light rain.'

Jake was more interested in how a man Jasper's age managed to work up that much ground, over two full acres, let alone seed it, and afterwards keep it weeded, and dusted for mites and weevils.

Jasper was pleased at this appreciation. 'You start early and you work late,' he explained. 'It helps that I don't have much else to do. I used to farm, the same as you and Rolfe Sumner do yet, but I sold out many years ago, and since then I've lived pretty much just to raise my grand-daughter. She's an orphan, you know.'

Jake didn't know, but neither did he ask. He had a glass of beer that Jasper had pressed upon him, and as they walked the garden near sundown, it was pleasant being there, with old Jasper, and capable of looking round now and then seeing Elizabeth through a wide kitchen window.

'Raising girls is something I could write a book about,' went on old Jasper. 'It's the dangdest undertaking a man could imagine. She's nigh to nineteen years old now, and that makes her a woman, but, Mister Bartlett, I can tell you she wasn't always this steady and placid.'

Jasper also reminisced about old Rolfe, about the First World War, about the village as it used to be when there were still horses and wagons on the roadways, about some of the colourful oldtimers who had been dead many years now, and in the end, shortly before Elizabeth called them inside to eat, Jasper took Jake out to his toolshed and showed him where he made homebrew beer in a warm and shady corner of the shed.

'Make a fresh batch about three times each summer. That's about all the weather will allow for. I used to make a batch or two in the house, in the pantry, in wintertime, because the pantry's got an even, warm temperature, but Liz's grandmother never liked that, especially after the last batch blew up on me and you could smell the stuff throughout the house for a month afterwards — and those were Prohibition days when Federal snoops were usually going round with their snouts in the air. Well, we'd better go in now and eat. I'm sure glad you could come tonight, Mister Bartlett. Being a man who has to look at womenfolk every mealtime, I'm proud to get to see a masculine face across from me for a change.'

Jasper's loquaciousness did not carry

over to mealtime. He was a believer in the New England edict that folks sat down to eat when they reached the table. Jake Bartlett liked old Jasper. He also showed appreciation when Elizabeth came back from taking the shine off her nose to join them at the table. She was an excellent cook, he said, and Liz brushed that off on the grounds that nothing was very exotic, or much of a challenge, when all that was involved was a beef roast.

Jake ate with a surprising appetite. Even Jasper, who did a fair share of outdoor labour, finally sat back and admired the younger man's capacity. It was, of course, a variety of homage to Liz's cooking, and that was how she took it; at the same time she was amazed. When it was time for her to get the dessert, Jake seemed to suddenly become aware that his host and hostess were covertly staring. He excused himself on the grounds that this was the best meal he had eaten in more than a year.

'Since I worked for a feed-lot company out in Nebraska.'

That was the first time he had ever mentioned working elsewhere before coming to Washington. Jasper was hard put not to use it as an opener to do a little prying, but from the other end of the table Liz's cool, hard stare kept him in check. Then Jake volunteered a little more, and both his companions listened with interest.

'They had a woman cook out there, which was unusual, and the food was almost as good as this meal has been. We fed out anywhere from ten to fifteen thousand head of beef every ninety days, it was hard work and the crew put in some long days, so maybe my uncle, who owned the place, figured the best way to keep good hands was to feed them well.'

Elizabeth went after the dessert, and in her absence her grandfather got in one question. 'Nebraska is a lot better farming country than Vermont; what-ever made you come here?'

The answer came easily and naturally. 'Well, my mother's people were from up here and I thought I'd like to see what it was like. So, here I am.' He grinned at Jasper. 'I love it. It's exactly as though I'd fallen through a slit in Time. It's like going back fifty years, even the band concert on the green on Independence Day. Even the size of the farms; the mountains and the forests, the creeks and rivers, and the apple orchards. It's Lilliput, but a more beautiful one than the original.' Jake stopped, looked narrowly at Jasper to see what reaction this sudden outburst had elicited, and when the older man nodded complacently, Jake made one last observation. 'This is where nothing matters but what is important to individual people. The values aren't mass-produced. Even the work is done by individuals *for* individuals, from shocking the hay to making the homebrew. It's a place where the basics really matter.'

Jasper may, and he may not, have

caught the gist of all this, but when Liz returned with their dessert plates and set them out, she smiled at Jake as though she hadn't missed anything even though she'd been out in the kitchen, and said, 'Mister Bartlett, you aren't going to get an argument out of the natives on your observations, but some of them,' she nodded towards her grandfather, 'aren't going to understand why you carry on so about individuality. That's all they've known all their lives. Whatever the world has turned into since they were young, is something they don't really believe.'

Jasper, with some idea he wasn't being made to look too good throughout all this, reared up and said, 'Liz, I read the newspaper just like everyone else. And watch television too.'

She smiled down the table. 'I'm not derogating you, Grandfather. My point is that the people of Washington have not been hurt nor upset nor really involved in anything that's happened in the world since the Second World War, and it's this insularity that has driven most of the younger ones away. Maybe the world is getting more sordid by the year, but people nowadays have to feel involved. Here, we just live as we've always lived.'

'What's wrong with that?' demanded old Jasper.

Jake tried being placating. 'Nothing at all. That's what I've been saying. It's a different world, and I love it. It's the way people should live, working with their hands, considering other people, letting their anxieties go hang.' Jake paused, then said, 'I've been considering buying a farm here and settling in Washington.'

That stopped the discussion dead. Old Jasper, who had been a farmer most of his life, liked the idea, although he probably wondered how a hired hand was going to pay for a farm, while his grand-daughter studied Jake silently for a while before she said, 'What will you miss the most, Mister Bartlett? Maybe you'd better stay through a winter before you make that decision.'

Jake laughed. 'I've been through winters as bad as anything Vermont can throw at me. But you are right, and I intend to do just that before buying.'

They finished their dessert and Jasper went to get the coffeepot to refill his own cup, and Jake's cup. Elizabeth declined. In fact, she excused herself and began clearing the table as her grandfather settled down again, interested in which farm Jake Bartlett might have in mind. Jasper ticked off half a dozen names, and said what he considered to be the shortcoming of each farm. Then Jake stopped him cold by saying he'd been thinking in terms of buying the Sumner place. Until Jasper remembered where Rolfe Sumner was, and what condition he was in, he shook his head.

'Rolfe would no more sell that place than he'd fly to the moon. It's been in his family since before the Rebellion.'

The idea had struck Jasper too suddenly, but a moment later he

66

recanted a little. 'Of course, with him ill and all . . . but even then, I wouldn't want to make a bet he'd sell. Rolfe is a very stubborn man.'

Jake did not press it. 'Well, there are other farms. I only mentioned the Sumner place because I'm familiar with it, have been running it by myself since Mister Sumner became ill.'

'Lots of other places,' agreed Jasper. 'Let me think it over for a few days. I used to know every farm within a hundred miles of town, what was wrong with 'em, which made a living, and which just broke folks one family after another.' Jasper arose from the table, his coffee cup emptied, his meal finished, and, for a change, his mind filled with something besides the yield, and the tribulations, of his garden patch.

Jake wanted to help Elizabeth clear up the dishes, but she was adamant and sent him to the parlour with her grandfather. Even so, it did not take long before she joined them. Jake told her again what a delightful meal it had been. She was pleased, but Jasper said, 'Pshaw, that was just one of her average suppers. You ought to be here when she really leans her heart into it, like at Christmas, and Thanksgiving Day. Her mother was a wonderful cook too. Handy in just about every way you could imagine.'

Something stopped old Jasper right there, probably a heartaching memory of Elizabeth's parents. He went silent for a long while, leaving Elizabeth and Jake to carry the conversation without him. They were equal to it. She was interested in his desire to settle in Vermont. He was interested in her, not exclusively as a cook, but also as a source of information. She somehow or other, and was never afterwards certain just how, found herself volunteering to show him some of the back-country, some of the forested hills and waterways.

He proved himself a capable man by driving her into a corner where she had to agree to go with him the very next Sunday. A little later, when he thought it was time for him to depart, she went outside upon the porch with him, a sweater cast round her shoulders, and he told her again it was the best dinner he'd had since he could remember. Then he took one of her hands and held it. 'And cooked by the prettiest woman ever.'

She freed the hand, but gently and amiably. 'You've been living alone up there at the Sumner place too long, Mister Bartlett. There are a dozen girls prettier than I am right here in the village.'

He didn't dispute it, but he did not look as though he either believed it or intended to go seek them out to be certain. He said he'd be driving in tomorrow to see Rolfe Sumner, to report on the livestock, the crops, the farm in general, because it seemed that old Rolfe lived from visit to visit, and if he might he'd like to drop by for a moment.

She was agreeable. The next day was Friday, and she baked every Friday morning, but the afternoons were free.

He hung there, on the porch, as though trying to make up his mind about something, but in the end he left with nothing more personal happening between them than that moment or two when he'd held her hand.

She returned to the parlour and found her grandfather sound asleep. She smiled; old Jasper led an even-paced life from morning until evening every day; nothing changed, nothing upset the serenity. Then, this evening, another man had appeared and her grandfather had drunk two cups of coffee, had eaten twice what he normally ate, and the result of this excitement was that he had fallen asleep in his chair.

She left him to return to the kitchen and do dishes. There was a lot for her to think about, too. Like her grandfather, life for Elizabeth Carleton was pretty much of a day-by-day orderly and peaceful existence. But tonight, something had happened that she couldn't define. It made her feel different, and even think differently. Jake Bartlett was a nice person, a farmhand who had done a very heroic thing. Naturally, folks would want to show him that they appreciated his quick thinking, Naturally.

But there was something else tied in with all that. She felt it, as though it were an instinct, but she could not define it even to herself, in private.

6

Jake Opens Up

When Jake arrived at Eulalia Wilson's place the following day shortly past noon, she greeted him with a warm smile and motioned for him to go out back. 'He's sitting out there under the apple tree,' she said, 'and he has a visitor: Elizabeth Carleton.'

Jake hadn't expected that. He'd had in mind going round to sit on the porch with Elizabeth a little later. When he passed down through the house and out back, and saw her sitting there in tree-shade with her tanned arms exposed and her body twisted in the chair while she listened to something old Rolfe was saying, he took down a shallow breath and let it out very slowly. She was beautiful. No way around it, Elizabeth Carleton was beautiful. He'd thought like that on the drive home last night, but without feeling very pleased about it.

Rolfe Sumner saw him and beckoned. Rolfe always perked up when his hired man arrived. Liz saw Jake striding across the yard also, and watched him with a soft smile. When he was close she said she'd meant to leave before this, so she'd be at home when he came by, but after delivering the garden produce she stopped to visit for a moment.

Throughout this explanation old Rolfe's faded eyes were narrow and shrewdly observing, but he said nothing until Jake greeted him, and pulled up a cane-bottomed old chair to join them beneath the boughs of the ancient apple tree.

'Everything is fine at the farm,' he told Rolfe. 'We could do with a light rain or two, but even so the grain is heading up nicely. I finished welding the teeth on the drill, so next summer it'll be ready at seeding time.'

For ten minutes they fired questions

and answers back and forth, practically ignoring Elizabeth, but she didn't seem to mind at all. She was interested in their technical conversations, or perhaps it was simply that she was interested in *them*.

Finally, Jake turned a smile her way, told old Rolfe about the superb dinner he'd had at the Carleton place the previous night, and concluded with a little laughing comment that Elizabeth's cooking had spoiled him for any other.

Rolfe was equal to that. 'I know they say there are chefs as can cook better than women, but I've never eaten anything a man cooked up that could hold a candle to women-cooked food. I think womenfolk put something into their cooking men cooks leave out — affection.' Rolfe smiled at Elizabeth. 'Affection for the family they cook for. Is that right?'

She laughed, and because they were both looking at her, she blushed. 'I couldn't reveal a professional secret,' she said. 'But there *is* something special.'

Their conversation was quiet but lively, and after a while Elizabeth arose to depart, which brought the two men to their feet. She said Jake could still drive by if he'd care to, and as they watched her walk across the grass towards the house, Rolfe Sumner sighed, sat back down, and said, 'If she only could have happened fifty years ago.' Then he seemed embarrassed by that and ducked his head as he swung an open hand at an annoying fly or gnat. 'I've been sitting round here thinking,' he said, as Jake also resumed his seat. 'I've got a house here in town that I rent. It's not much, but it's adequate. I've been thinking that maybe, after I'm well enough to leave Eulalia's place, I probably ought to settle in down there for a while. At least through the winter. In case I have a set-back, or something like that, it'd be a lot handier to help.'

Jake sat quietly, looking very relieved.

'Sounds like a good idea,' he conceded. 'At least until next summer. There's no point in being out at the farm through the winter anyway.'

Rolfe said, 'No,' and paused after saying it to gaze at his companion. 'Don't suppose you'd be interested in staying on. You men leave right after the autumn harvest, not that I blame you; certainly isn't anything much to be done around here come wintertime.'

Jake surprised the old man. 'I might be interested, Mister Sumner. To tell you the truth, I've about decided to settle here in Washington. I mentioned buying a farm to Mister Carleton last night.'

Rolfe pursed his lips and looked long at Jake Bartlett. 'It's not a growing community,' he warned. 'Washington's a good place to die in, but was I your age I'm not too sure I'd want to spend the rest of my life here.'

To that Jake simply said, 'We differ. Maybe it's in what life means to us. I like it here as well as any place I've ever

76

been, and better than most places.' He stood up. The afternoon was half spent and if he stopped by the Carleton place too, it was going to make him a little late getting back to the farm. 'I'll bring you in a few heads of the oats tomorrow or Monday, Mister Sumner, so you can see how they are heading up.'

Rolfe smiled. He would like that. There was one field at the farm that as far as Rolfe could remember had never been planted to anything but oats. For the past fifteen or so years it had been necessary to use commercial fertiliser, but before that the field had turned in a good yield every year as dependable as clockwork, unless of course it happened to be a drought springtime.

After Jake left, Rolfe went into the house to look for Eulalia. He wanted to tell her that unless he was 'way off in his calculations, Jake Bartlett was seeing Elizabeth Carleton with something more in his mind than an occasional free supper.

It was a good guess. When Jake

parked Rolfe's car out front and Elizabeth waved to him from a flowerbed where she had been weeding, he walked on over with an admiring look. Liz looked like more woman at nineteen than most women looked at thirty. When she straightened up in her old faded gardening dungarees and her sleeveless white blouse, and raised a hand to push away a coil of taffy hair, she said, 'Did you see Eulalia before you left?' and when Jake shook his head Liz said, 'Well, you should have. I think Rolfe had another slight tremor last night. She said something like that to me when I met her out front on my way home.' Liz put aside her green plastic gloves and her weeding tools, took him up to the porch in the blessed shade, and each one of them sat in an old rocker as she said, 'I wonder how long he can go on like that? He looks healthy enough, most of the time. But I'm no authority, and I stopped by Aggie's library this afternoon and got a book on heart trouble. I read a couple of chapters before it got too depressing, then I came out here to fight weeds.'

'What did it say?' he asked.

'That any attack can be fatal, and the chances after the second or third attack increase tremendously that the next seizure *will* be fatal.'

Jake did not seem surprised. 'I hope he can go in his sleep. It's always seemed to me that that is the way it should be arranged for people like Rolfe Sumner to go. Decent people.'

She turned. 'Jake, tell me frankly, do you know anything about medicine?'

He considered her for a moment, then nodded. 'I know as much as a medical aidman in the army ever learns. But heart attacks are pretty darned rare among soldiers whose average ages are somewhere around twenty-two to twenty-eight.' He rocked a moment, then said, 'Want a confidence, Liz?'

He had never used that nickname before, but it sounded so natural the quiet way he said it that she did not notice.

She replied cautiously, 'I don't know whether I'm up to it, Jake. Am I?'

'You're a grown woman,' he said soberly. 'Someday you'd have to know anyway.' He rocked a little more, then stopped the chair from moving. 'I lost seven soldiers entrusted to me in Viet Nam, seven wounded men. I did what I could and it wasn't enough. I should have been able to save them.'

She said, 'Should you? Isn't a medical aidman a sort of nurse? What could you have done with limited training, Jake?'

'That's the point, Liz, I had more than limited training. I had three years of medical training at the University of Oregon. I was studying to be a doctor when the army called me up. I had more than limited training. Do you see?'

She didn't see, but she understood one thing; he had lived with this torment for a long while, had taken it with him everywhere he went, and she also began to understand something else about him; he was one of those men who had to find release working with their hands, using their backs and muscles to help blank out their thoughts. She had never believed for a moment he was a typical hired farmhand.

'I tried to save each one of them and they slipped away, one by one. I knew all seven of them. They were friends of mine, from the same outfit. I could tell you their names and where they were from.'

'What good would that do?' she asked quickly, recognising that something was boiling up out of him that had to be dammed up again, had to be stopped. 'Jake, how can you possibly blame yourself?'

'I told you, Liz. Because I should have been able to save every one of them. That's why the medics left them in my care. I was qualified, better qualified than any other medic around, excluding the doctors, and they were gone to the rear where hospitals were.

My job was to keep those seven going until I could get them back. When I arrived I brought with me seven corpses.'

She wanted to say something comforting, but couldn't think what it should be. Better to say nothing than to be inane. She prayed that her grandfather would not come ambling round from out back, and at least this prayer was answered, but not the one asking for guidance, so she sat there with him, feeling helpless.

'I'll tell you something about war,' he said, after a long silence. 'It doesn't leave you with anything. No dreams, no prayers answered, no illusions. And it can happen anywhere, any time. It doesn't break your spirit, it warps it, and it doesn't destroy *you*, just your confidence in yourself.'

Now she had something to say. 'Jake, you have enough confidence. You know exactly what to do and when to do it. Rolfe Sumner said you were the most capable hired man he'd ever seen.'

Jake laughed hollowly. 'That's part of my running, Liz. That's part of my closed-mind strategy. I keep busy all the while and that way I don't remember. As for knowing; my folks were well-off farmers in Kansas and Nebraska. I learned all the tricks before I was out of high-school. How to weld, how to pull a tractor block and overhaul the motor, how to do all the usual work on a farm. Then I went to war, and since then — here and there, until I found this place. Here, it's possible to pretend none of that other stuff ever happened. This isn't even in the same century, is it?'

She understood, now, why he had said some of the things she'd heard him say about the village, about the band on Independence Day, about people mattering here as individuals. 'It's the same century,' she said softly. 'How long ago did that happen, Jake?'

'Four years ago.'

'You were a boy then.'

'Once you've aimed a gun at

someone and pulled the trigger, you aren't a boy, Liz. Don't make excuses for me. That's not necessary. The facts are there — it all happened just one way. Alibis might have helped if even some of them had made it. But not when all seven of them got away from me.'

Jake pushed up to his feet and the chair behind him rocked emptily. He turned and said, 'I don't know what in the hell possessed me to tell you this today. I thought, last night on the drive back to the farm, that maybe I'd tell you on Sunday, when we had all day and I could make it seem mitigated some way.'

She arose. 'Jake, don't things like that happen in war? Isn't that what war is — the most dehumanising experience people can pass through; something that leaves scars on their souls even when they are innocent? What possible good can come from blaming yourself for something that happened four years ago, and that you tried to prevent and simply could not stop from happening?'

'That's it, Liz. I had the knowledge. I should have been able to prevent it.'

'Well, evidently you *didn't* have the knowledge, Jake, if you tried hard and still failed.'

He started to speak, then bit it off and blew out a big breath instead. 'I'll be by for you in the morning, tomorrow, all right?'

She nodded. 'All right. Is there any particular part of the countryside you'd like to see?'

He said, 'No, not really. And I'm sorry for upsetting you like this. I didn't intend to, not today anyway.' He stepped close, felt for her fingers, squeezed, and she squeezed back, then he trotted down the steps and out to the car. As he drove off, this time, he waved, and she returned it. Then a thought struck her. There was more to his dilemma than he had told her; there had to be, because Jake Bartlett was not the kind of man to carry something haunting around with him for four years unless it was more solidly based in his conscience than this thing, as he had explained it to her, had any right to be.

7

Sunday Morning

Sunday in backwoods New England meant an early breakfast, followed by about two hours of church, but Elizabeth excused herself to her grandfather on the basis that what she had to do today couldn't be put off, and Jasper did not argue about it. Lately, he'd found her reasoning to be as sound as new money, and that gratified him a lot. Native New Englanders put a lot of store in good common-sense logic, although as a rule they did not expect it from beautiful girls.

Jasper was gone by the time Jake arrived, looking shiny-faced and fresh. He had even washed Rolfe Sumner's car, and dusted out the inside, which was a good idea since Rolfe not only never washed a car, leaving that to the rain, but he used them to haul all manner of equipment parts and feed sacks, until they resembled a truck.

Liz came out to meet him in a fresh pair of blue trousers and a lighter blue sleeveless shirt over which she had a light sweater. She was wearing lace-boots and had her taffy hair held firmly in place by a wide blue ribbon. She looked ready to go exploring in a jungle, fit and prepared for anything.

He smiled as he held the car door for her. 'Where's your rifle?'

She screwed up her face at him, waited until the door was closed, then got comfortable on the front seat. As he slid in opposite her she looked him up and down, and nodded. 'You dressed for it too, didn't you?'

He agreed. 'Yes. But I haven't the least idea what 'it' is.'

'Head up into town and take the first road west and I'll show you what 'it' is.'

He laughed and left the kerbing prepared to make a circle of the square. She corrected him at the last moment so that they would avoid passing up through town. It was Sunday, she explained, bad enough for her to be seen dressed for an outing when she should be at church, but worse to look as though she were enjoying it.

The road west, or left, from town went arrow-straight for several miles and was visible every inch of the way, until it rose to breast a low swale and drop down the far side. After that, with a few farmed fields on each side of the road, but with more and more stands of timber intervening, they were heading towards the rugged back-country of Vermont that woodsmen and hunters explored each autumn, but few other people did unless there was a camping ground near the road, or perhaps one of the beautiful little upland lakes. It was one of the latter that was their destination, but Liz said nothing of this until they were cruising far beyond town in a world of forest-shapes and forest-shadows. The scent of fir and pine and spruce was strong on a warm day because the sap melted and moved best at such a time. There were birds of various kinds, squirrels, and even a few deer, once they were well away from the last habitation. By the time they arrived where a pair of what looked to Jake like wagon-ruts meandered to their right from the paved road, and Liz told him to turn off there, he was beginning to feel that she not only knew exactly where she was going, but that she knew this countryside very well, for a girl.

He eased down into second range and went gingerly over the old ruts. She smiled at his caution, and he explained it by reminding her that the car did not belong to him.

The ruts wound round and through pine groves so thick in places no sunlight ever reached the needle-bouyant earth. Kansas, where he had grown up, was as flat as a dinner-plate, and even neighbouring Nebraska, at least the parts he knew best, had nothing more than grassy, rolling prairies. This, he told her, was like exploring New England for the first time.

She told him to stop, when they reached a wide clearing where someone a very long while previous had dropped two immense firs across the ruts, barring access by vehicle very effectively. From there on they walked, she leading and setting a brisk pace. There was not very much said on the trail. It was steep in places, and in other places it was gloomy dark and hushed, unconducive to conversation.

Only when she stopped beside a white-water creek did he move up close, studying the onward country, and said, 'I thought I saw a longhouse up ahead with some Iriquois sitting round outside in warpaint sharpening their weapons.'

She laughed, sank down to drink at the creek, and when he dropped down at her side, she waited until he had tanked up, then reared back on her haunches and waited until he was finished before speaking.

'Where we're going there used to be a longhouse, in fact, but I don't think they were Iriquois. I've forgotten what they were. Anyway, nothing remains. My grandfather saw old ovens and some graves and a few remains of long shanties, when he was a boy, but it's all gone now.'

'Then why go there?' he asked, wiping water off his chin. She jumped up. 'Come along and I'll show you.'

It wasn't much farther, another mile or mile and a half, and when he finally caught sight of the lake through the trees it was easy to understand why someone would want to drive and trudge this far.

They emerged where a little creek ran between two immense, lichen-covered old rocks to empty into the lake. But there would have to be a dozen or more other little creeks doing the same thing, if surface water was the source, because the lake looked Jake to be about a mile long and at least once again that wide. It was bluish with a greeny overtone from the shoreline-forested reflection. Trees grew right down to the water's edge, and except for several obviously man-made clearings of respectable size, the forest completely surrounded it.

Some mallards took wing the moment the people appeared, and several immense Canadian honkers at the far end, alarmed by the ducks, also fled, but it took them longer to get airborne and in the process they came beating down the lake to within a hundred yards of the man and girl before lifting off. She looked at Jake. 'Do you wish you had a rifle?'

He watched the geese rise and form their flying wedge, and shook his head. 'No. I've had all the killing a man needs for one lifetime.'

She took him to one of the clearings where grass and weeds grew amid a profusion of wild flowers. On the directly opposite bank was another clearing of roughly the same size. This, she explained, was where the Indians had lived, half the band on this side, half the band on the far side of the lake, and in that way, it was thought, if there was no crowding, there would be no feuding. She wondered if it had worked.

He thought that it had. 'If you lived over there, and I lived here, I'd paddle over in my canoe to visit you, but not too often, and you wouldn't run me off.'

She laughed, and showed him where her grandfather had once showed her, when she'd been twelve years old, where the old graves were, but now there wasn't so much as a mound of earth left. Grass grew, flowers nodded; if there had been markers, stones mounded into cairns, or perhaps totems of upright wood, there was no sign of them now. He thought that was as it should be.

'Their way of life is gone. They should be allowed to go with it, otherwise college students under the guise of amateur archaeologists would have come up here and dug them out to sift through the bones for artifacts.' He leaned upon an ancient fir. 'Let the dead rest in peace; they have earned it.'

She knew how his thoughts were running. Without even knowing him that well, she could tell from his brooding eyes what was bothering him now. She took him by the hand and tugged him on through the trees to a place where someone, perhaps centuries ago, had created a kind of stone rip-rap on both sides of a small creek, forcing the water to flow perfectly straight for something like a hundred feet before it rose enough to clear a small stone weir and flow into the lake.

He dropped to his knees beside the weir and beckoned for her to kneel with him. Then he pointed into the clear water. 'Keep your shadow from frightening them.' She saw four large, fat trout lying in the eddy behind the weir-stones. He lowered his arm. 'Whoever he was, the man who planned and engineered this fishtrap, he was no ignorant savage. Look, all I've got to do is block their escape up-creek by jumping in behind them, then I lean forward with both hands, and when they frantically rise to swim over the weir-stones, I scoop them up on to the grass. I wonder how many times he did that and brought food home for supper?'

Liz's grandfather had explained it the same way. She was too wise, though, to say as much. She let Jake Bartlett make this discovery all by himself. As they arose and cast long shadows, the luggard trout took fright, rose, and flashed like wet steel as they dived across the stones and sank on the far side where the lake waited.

The sun was stalking across a spotless sky, but there were still shadows and plenty of places to escape from the heat. Jake wished they had brought a picnic lunch and their bathing suits. Liz hadn't been sure he'd like the lake all that much, but those things had been in her mind the evening before. What had deterred her had been some vague idea that as soon as she had shown him the lake they would go back and drive somewhere else. Now though, he seemed as content as possible, and after exploring the clearing on the west side of the lake he struck out to hike round to the other clearing, on the east side. She followed, perfectly content that he had usurped the initiative. It really wasn't a woman's place, anyway, exploring lakes and forests.

The other clearing, however, was even more barren of any trace of the people who had lived there, had cleared the land, probably for many generations, and Jasper hadn't ever showed Elizabeth anything of note over there, so after walking round the clearing and across it, Jake took her down to the water's edge where a punky old deadfall pine lay quietly rotting in a spongy mass of shoreline grass and reeds, and sat her down, to watch for fish with him.

'How many Indians, I wonder?' he

said. 'It's not that big a lake. When there got to be too many and it strained the resources, what did they do — draw lots to see which ones migrated?'

She thought of the village when she replied. 'No. When the venturesome younger ones got bored, they packed up and struck out on their own. There are dozens of other lakes farther back in the mountains. Maybe each little group started its own settlement like that, and came back every few years to visit the old folks.'

He considered that, turned and looked amiably at her. 'I like your combination of imagination and — well — hope, that everything worked out well for them.'

'There are other clearings around the other lakes. When I was growing up, after my parents were killed, my grandfather, bless him, used to hike me all over these mountains in the hope that I'd be interested and stop brooding. When I think back to how I repaid his patience, I dislike myself. He was so endlessly good with me. He taught me to fish, and to identify most of the birds and little animals. I know at times I nearly drove him to distraction.' Liz sighed, and watched a sleek brown trout nose cautiously into the shadows seeking food. As long as she did not move, the fish would pay her little attention. 'The worst part of it, Jake, is that while I was being mean and selfish, I knew I was hurting him, and yet I went right ahead and did it.'

'We hurt whom we love,' he said, and also watched the trout. 'I don't suppose there is really any way to mature without being something you never want to be, for a while at least. Maybe the secret is to know when to stop being that unlikeable person.' He moved a hand to ward off a mosquito, and the trout swapped ends in a flash and sped into deep water, leaving only a vague bit of stirred sediment to show that he had been there at all. 'I'm twenty-five,' he said, 'and I can tell you from experience that life is a constant contest; the ones who can't manage it do pointless and cruel things. I used to know a man in the army who had to make a play for every girl he saw, married or unmarried, and when he was successful he'd brag to anyone who would listen. It used to make me wonder if he really would ever realise that somewhere, back down his earlier years, his emotional structure had stopped maturing at a very young age. He couldn't cope with life unless he could brag that he'd made a conquest; he was an emotional seven-year-old.'

Elizabeth knew the type, not in men but in women. She also thought that Jake's brooding temperament made him deeper, more reflective, than any other man she had ever known. She had to decide whether she liked that or not.

Then she arose from the deadfall-log and beckoned for him to follow her on the path back to the car. 'We have one more stop to make today.'

He did not insist on knowing. They went back the way they had come, but just before the lake was lost to sight through the trees, he turned and looked back. 'Peaceful,' he said, and resumed walking.

She set a steady pace on the return trip, that was just a notch or two faster than the pace she'd set on their way to the lake, but mostly, on the way back, the trail was downhill, and that helped.

They stopped again for a drink of water at the creek, and in about one-half the time it had taken to walk upwards from the car, they were back to it again.

8

Sunday Evening

She directed him almost back to the village again, then she had him approach from the rear and glide down through town by the back-streets until they were at her home, and there she took him inside where she found a note from her grandfather saying he'd gone over to visit with Eulalia and Rolfe, and might not be back in time for lunch. He wasn't.

She sat Jake down in the kitchen, made him a cold plate with enormous slices of cold roast beef on it, tossed him a salad, and, instead of coffee, she made him chilled tea. It was a large lunch, and fed to him in large portions, and he ate every bit of it without a second glance. All Elizabeth had was a Golden Delicious apple and a glass of

cold water. She wasn't a weight-watcher
— yet, anyway — but she seldom ate in
the middle of the day, and when she
did, she ate no more than she was
eating now. Eventually, when Jake was
nearly finished, he saw what her
luncheon consisted of, and shook his
head as he arose to clear the kitchen
table with her. 'You can't keep up your
strength eating like that, Liz. If you
want to put in a good day's work you've
got to fortify yourself for it.'

'Is that your secret — eat like a horse
then work like one, too, to burn the
energy?'

He started washing the dishes as he
agreed. 'Correct. Turn in an honest
day's work on honest food.'

She leaned, reached over and turned
off the water and pushed him gently
away from the sink. 'No one, least of all
a man, does dishes in my kitchen,
without my invitation. Anyway, we still
have some more exploring to do. It's
only slightly past noon.'

He dried his hands. 'I could have

taken you to lunch in town somewhere. I don't have to mooch off you for every meal when we are together.'

She herded him out of her kitchen and back to the front porch where some strolling neighbours in their Sunday-best looked up just in time to see Elizabeth push him out of the house. Their scrubbed, shiny faces reflected shock, and after they had strolled on Liz said, 'Well, there went my good reputation.'

Jake was embarrassed, which she hadn't intended, so she smiled as they went out to the car. 'Don't worry. It may all turn out for the best. I know what they've been saying this past summer.' She screwed up her face to imitate one of the older village women and said, in a very prim tone of voice, 'Hmmmph! There's that Carleton girl lives down there with her grandfather, and doesn't go out much with boys. Mark my word, that's an unhealthy life for a young girl. She's going to wind up being a spinster, sure as the good Lord made green apples. Humph!'

Jake laughed and held the door for her. 'Liz, there is no chance, no chance under the sun, of you ending up a spinster. Even old Mister Sumner said yesterday that if you had happened fifty years earlier he'd have wed you himself, and that is quite a concession from a seventy-year-old confirmed bachelor. It sure surprised me.'

She looked soft-eyed for a moment, thinking about old Rolfe Sumner. Then she brisked up, determined that nothing was going to happen that would push Jake into his brooding frame of mind again. 'Drive southward this time,' she said, 'and for heaven's sake be sure we have enough gasoline. It could be a long walk back.'

He thought they had plenty providing she did not have in mind driving out of the state, but he did not ask her where she was taking him. He acted as he had earlier in the day — as though, if she wanted it to be a surprise, he would do nothing to hinder that.

Below the village two miles she told him to take the easterly cut-off, and after that, although they passed farms by the score, there was no traffic. The reason, she said, was because the Sunday dinner in New England was a traditional affair with all the family gathered after church, still attired in their ties and suit-coats. He knew; back home in Nebraska his mother had told him of those New England Sunday dinners when she'd been a child.

That offered Liz an opportunity, so she asked about him, about his parents, his home, his childhood and young manhood. 'All I know about you really, Jake, is that you are a good man in an emergency.'

He shot her a look. 'You know more, Liz. You learned more last night.'

She hadn't meant for this to come up again just yet, so she tried skirting around it. 'But tell me about home in Nebraska.'

'Not much to tell. My parents own four large farms. I have an older brother, Jim, who manages two of them. My father manages the other two. I never really wanted to be a farmer; at least, not their kind of a farmer where you fly between farms in your airplane and supervise working crews until there is no personal reality connected with it at all. I guess all my life I've wanted to be an individual among other individuals. That's why I fell in love with your village, I suppose.' He paused and looked at her. 'I didn't rebel, if that's what you're thinking, Liz. I just told them, after I got home from the war, that I was going away and that maybe someday when I found myself, I'd come back. My father and brother understood, I think. My mother wept a little and gave me thirty thousand dollars, her savings.'

Liz was astonished. 'Jake, that's an awful lot of money.'

He nodded. 'I sent it back the first city I stopped in. How do you find yourself if the way is greased for you?'

'You should go back, though,' opined

Liz. 'If for no other reason than to let them know you are all right.'

He said, 'Someday, but there's no hurry. I write them every couple of weeks. It's not that they are enemies or that I resent them; I think the world of all three of them. It's just that I don't want my brother's life, which is what I'd end up with if I went back and stayed there.'

They were approaching a steel bridge across a wide river. There was a sign urging drivers to drive slowly across the bridge. Jake slowed, leaned out to look at the river, and waved to someone below who was looking up. It was a young boy fishing from the shore. He waved back and Jake laughed. 'He knows who he is, doesn't he?'

Liz smiled. 'He probably also knows that when he sneaks home he's due for a tanning for sneaking out after church. Turn left up ahead, Jake, and climb the mountain.'

It was actually a hill, a bluff that was mustardy coloured above the wide old river, but the road to the top was steep. It had a stone watering trough mid-way up, and there were several lay-bys, flat places left over from an earlier time when teamsters had had to stop and 'blow' their horses several times before reaching the top. Liz's grandfather had told her one time that when the road was finished the drayage men around town had threatened to lynch the builder for making the road so steep, and yet it was hard to see how he could have done otherwise, because the bluff, although thick and high and bulky, was not very wide, thus there had been no feasible way to bank and turn the road to alleviate the steepness.

To a car it made no difference. They scooted on up to the last lay-by, and saw a young couple parked there, shoulder-to-shoulder in blissful silence. They drove right on past, neither of them commenting, as they had about the young boy with the fishing pole back down beneath the old trestle-bridge, and a hundred or so yards beyond emerged atop the bluff where sunshine hit down hard, making the heat very noticeable because there was not so much as a shrub growing up there, let alone any trees to stand beneath. Also, while the sun was low enough down the westerly sky to allow for long shadows in some places below, up atop the bluff it still shone as brightly as ever.

They left the car and walked over where a series of cement pilings, in which were set large lengths of black pipe, kept sightseers from getting too close to the abrupt drop off. Below, several hundred feet, was the river, and on their left was the steel bridge. If the youthful fisherman was still down there, he was not visible.

Northwestward lay the village, in its ancient and quaint tree-shaded setting, and elsewhere were the farms, the outlying residences, stone fences and farmed fields stretching as far as the enfolding hills and mountains would allow. It was, without question, the best view of Washington and the entire watershed-area, the entire wide valley, to be had. Climbing some backdrop mountain would give a greater scope, but it would not show as much in detail, and in fact it probably wouldn't show the village at all because of the trees.

Liz gestured calmly. 'There is your town, Mister Bartlett, and if you'll trace out the north roadway and look closely you'll be able to make out the chimney and roofline of the Sumner place.'

While he stood looking, Liz did what she usually did when she came up here, she tried to find the Carleton house at the lower end of town. It wasn't very difficult, once a person got a good bearing and sighted over some in-line treetops.

Jake sighed and leaned on the guard-pipe. 'It's like a picture from a story book when you're a little kid. Red barns; little, white-painted two-storey houses with old-fashioned curlicues under the eaves; tree-lined old streets, and a village green with a cannon in it. It's like . . . ' He looked at her. 'I'm not making fun of it, Liz.'

She smiled. 'I understand. I've often thought the same way. You called it Lilliput, and since then I've thought that was very appropriate.'

'I hope it never changes,' he said, with soft fervour.

'Something will have to happen first,' she said. 'A factory will have to come, or someone will have to devise some kind of commercial enterprise that will feed money into the economy. Otherwise it's going to go the next hundred years probably very little different than it's come the past three hundred.' She turned to face him. 'What about boredom, Jake? That's what's driven all the young people away.'

He shook his head. 'Not much chance. But if it happened, what's to stop people from going on a trip for a few weeks? The issue with me, Liz, is that I don't have to rush forth in search of the world. I've found it. I've been out there and seen it at its best and its worst, and all either did for me was drive me away in search of basic things, in search of myself and a place like Washington, Vermont, where being myself is enough. Okay?'

She said, 'Okay. I'm not trying to discourage you. I'm only trying to help you be certain.'

He kept looking at her. 'Liz, I left something out last night.'

She had thought this would be the proper place, so now she braced herself, but in soft silence. This was his time, not hers.

'I drank. After the doctors pulled out and left me with those seven wounded, and thirty Montagnards, those Vietnamese mountain people, to start the long haul back to the base, I kept myself going on whisky. I was drugged on the stuff most of the way back, numb on it. If there'd been anything better I'd have taken that, too.'

She was surprised because he was not a weakling. Fright might have possessed him, but she knew him well enough now to realise that he did not react in emergencies with fear and trembling. She'd seen him saving a life and he'd been as calm, as brisk and capable as anyone could possibly be.

'Why?' she asked.

'Thirty-six hours on the line, Liz, without very much to eat and no sleep at all. Binding them up, easing some to the other side, even lying in the mud fighting like the others when I had to. Rum-dumb; out on my feet, but the whisky seemed to keep my nerves from crawling outside my skin; it made it possible for me to function like a zombie, but to function. It also made me incapable of being properly observant. I saw men bleeding and did nothing about it. It was as though the best thing that could happen to them would be to die and get the hell out of it — out of *all* of it.'

She caught her lower lip between her teeth and held it. He kept looking at her, but in a way he was looking through her to something else far in the distance, something he could not take his eyes off.

'You see; a drunk medic walking ahead of his stretcher-bearers like a zombie, and when the Montagnards would call I just told them to shut up and keep marching, that we had to get to base hospital. I didn't stop, and I should have. The Montagnards knew it, but I was the leader. I walked nine miles, then found a truck convoy and loaded in my men and rode the rest of the way, with the whisky bottle in my lap. When I unloaded at the base, there they were, seven corpses.'

She waited, when he stopped, to see if he would say more, but he didn't. He'd said it all, had purged himself to her. She leaned on the railing, unmindful of the late-day heat, visualising a horror she never would have imagined by herself, and feeling a little sick as she did so.

A car came up the hill, slowed on the top-out, then picked up speed and went hurrying on down the far, northward side of the bluff. That was the only thing that broke the stillness where she stood with him, until, an hour or so later, he said they had ought to go back now, that it was evening or close to it, and he'd brought in some oat-heads in a sack for Rolfe, over at Eulalia's house.

9

A Woman's Instinctive Knowledge

When he left her on the porch and started back to the car, she stopped him with a soft call, then ran out where he was in the late-day shadows and said, 'Listen to me, Jake, there are limits for all of us. How many others could have even kept going the full thirty-six hours?'

He looked down into her tilted face. 'There were others who did. Not medics, maybe, and without the same responsibilitity, but they kept slugging it out until they broke the back of an offensive. Those seven who died were that kind.' He reached and gently pushed back a coil of taffy hair that was hanging loosely on her forehead. 'Liz, don't make excuses for me. I've thought of them all, every damned one, and all they make me feel like is some kind of lousy hypocrite.'

'But thirty-six hours, Jake, without sleep . . . '

'That's a mitigating factor,' he conceded. 'Now alibi the whisky and the neglect of my men; can you do that for me, too? I don't think so, Liz. Like I just said, I've tried them all and it still comes out the same way — when I really was needed, I couldn't stand up to it. Hell, anyone would have done what I did for Mister Sumner when he needed oxygen, providing they knew what to do. That wasn't heroic, that was a natural reaction to an emergency by someone trained to do exactly what he did.' Jake smiled. 'And I had no right burdening you with this mess, either, except that you are — special — and under those circumstances you deserved to know.' He shifted position as though anxious to be on his way, and this time she let him go.

Afterwards, when his car was no longer visible, and up and down her street there was silence and stillness, she retreated as far as the porch and sat down on the top step, to try and sift through what she knew.

In former times she'd had a ready-made solution to all her problems; she could run to her grandfather, and because he had lived so long and had seen so much, he not only usually had a solution, he was never very upset, and that had its calming effect upon her.

But this was different. She couldn't go to him with Jake Bartlett's confidence. She couldn't go to anyone, yet she sat there hugging her knees thinking that of all the people on earth who were incapable of resolving something this difficult, she was probably first and foremost. She was one of the Lilliputians Jake laughed about, one of the protected, insular people to whom life was a series of changing seasons and little else.

After a while she went indoors because it was time to make her grandfather's supper. She had absolutely no appetite at all, and so great was her preoccupation that she had reached the kitchen before it dawned on her that her grandfather hadn't been sitting in the parlour. She went back to switch on some lights and be sure. He wasn't; he was probably still down at Eulalia's visiting with Rolfe Sumner.

In a way she was relieved at that possibility, and went to the kitchen to make supper without being distracted from her gloominess.

The telephone rang once. It was Agatha Thorpe wanting to know if Jasper was home, and when Liz said he wasn't, and where she thought Agatha could reach him, the older woman said, 'That's a fine-looking young man, Elizabeth. I'm speaking of young Jake Bartlett.'

Liz sighed to herself. The talk had already started. 'He's good company,' she told Agatha Thorpe, and terminated the conversation.

He *was* good company, too. He had a

handsome smile and a lilting laugh. He was nice to be with, and easy to be around. He never took advantage of things and never seemed to be other than perfectly natural — except for when he fell into a brooding mood. At first she hadn't noticed, but now she knew, the moment he started turning quiet and pensive, what it was, and as she worked over supper for her grandfather, she noticed in herself a similar propensity; after all, what he felt himself guilty of was no very slight nor insignificant thing. She couldn't very well brood about it and not show the same kind of reaction.

But she finally decided to take the offensive. Thirty-six hours without sleep impaired even the strongest men until their judgement was unreliable. Also, *she* knew, if no one else seemed to have thought of it, that Jake Bartlett was gentle and thoughtful; he was not a killer, either for an ideal or for anything else. Jake Bartlett was not a soldier. Some men were, some men could not be. Jake had done his duty and he had done more than others had a right to expect of him, while all the while he was not psychologically suited to warfare, to killing, to living in filth and degradation, like a mad animal.

That, perhaps more than the thirty-six sleepless hours, was what had accounted for the whisky and the constant haze that came out of it for Jake. He had reached his limit. He had stopped functioning as a soldier and had started functioning as exactly what he had called himself — a zombie, a moving, talking, marching robot incapable of thought and organised mental reactions. He had gone as far as he could psychologically go, and from there on he had been travelling on nerve and reflex. And seven wounded men had died.

They probably would have died anyway, some of them. Stretcher cases in wartime suffer the worst kind of shock. She had read one time something written by an eminent doctor about people dying more often from the shock of being mangled in car smashes and wars than ever died from their actual injuries.

The front door opened and closed and she hadn't even heard her grandfather stomping up the steps, which she usually could hear on a quiet evening even when she was in the kitchen.

She waited for him to come to the back of the house, and he did, after a while; came in, nodded soberly at her, went to the floor-to-ceiling cupboard-cooler and dug round for a bottle of scotch he kept hidden there, and when he had it he mixed the scotch into a glass of milk and took the glass to the kitchen table and sat down with it. He looked up at Elizabeth and said, 'Rolfe went this evening.' Then he took several swallows from the glass while she stood at the drainboard, stunned.

'I sat with him this afternoon out under the apple tree,' mused old Jasper in a husky, slow-dragging voice. 'We recalled a lot of things from 'way back.

It was a nice visit. One of the best I ever had with him. Directly, young Jake Bartlett came in, kind of quiet, and had some oat-heads in a paper sack for Rolfe to see how well the crop was doing. Rolfe was pleased as he could be. The three of us sat around for a spell talking about farming, then Eulalia came and told Rolfe it was time for his bath.' Jasper drank some more from his glass of milk and scotch. 'Rolfe stood up and started to say something to us. He got a strange look on his face, then he faced young Bartlett and said, 'Good luck, son. If I'd had a boy, you would have been him.' And he fell forward. Jake caught him, and I helped ease him back down in the chair. Eulalia came running. Rolfe was dead, Elizabeth. Just like that. 'Good luck, son,' he said, and died so easy I couldn't believe it. He didn't look dead at all, just resting-like.'

Elizabeth had to grope for her handkerchief to stem the flow of silent tears while her grandfather finished his scotch and milk looking out the back window far, far beyond where any young person could have seen, without saying another word.

Supper was out of the question. Jasper went to mix himself another of those unique drinks of his and Liz went to telephone over and ask Eulalia if there was anything she could do. Jake had just left, Eulalia said, the least disorganised person of them all, and it was a wonderful thing that Rolfe had been able to see Jake before he went, because he thought so much of him. But no, there wasn't much Liz could do; in the morning they would call for Rolfe's body in the hearse, and he would be buried the day after tomorrow at the old village cemetery where his forebears had been buried for generations. Rolfe was the last of them.

Elizabeth rang off, went back to the kitchen to put things away, and her grandfather was getting a little colour into his slack, grey face, finally. She felt a premonition about him drinking two glasses of that mixture, but said nothing. There was a time for a woman to speak her mind, and there was a time for her to keep her thoughts to herself. This was one of the latter times.

They somehow got through the rest of the evening, and each in their own way breathed a prayer for Rolfe before retiring. It took the passage of time, and that alone, to assuage the sensation of loss that came with death. Sleep helped, but, more than that, it took time; days and, depending upon the closeness, weeks and months, and sometimes years.

The following morning they each had a cup of coffee, then Jasper made a suggestion: 'Suppose we drive out to the Sumner place. Jake was hard hit by it, and we're about the only close friends he has around the village.'

Elizabeth was agreeable. They got into Jasper's old car and made the drive with a large, orange sun opposing them with its glare most of the way. Once they left the village, where tree-shade impeded the brilliance, there was very little shelter from the glare for most of the way because as a rule rural people, while fond of trees round their buildings, could not abide them in their farmed fields, and that included the roadway or beside it.

But the heat was in abeyance. It would not come until close to noon. In fact, the morning was still and beautiful, the way most mid-summer early mornings are. The sky was pale and flawless, there was a soft stillness to the countryside, and even with the sun up there promising heat later in the day, as they turned off the county road heading up Sumner Lane towards the old-fashioned two-storey house, there was a sweetness to the morning Elizabeth would always remember.

Jake saw them coming. He was washing the tractor with a small bottle with an attached nozzle attached to the garden hose. The bottle contained gasoline. It mixed with the water and under hose-pressure the mixture very effectively cut through oil and grease and tractor-grime. He was finishing this job when they stopped and alighted. He smiled, went to turn off the water, then dug out a large wiping-rag from a dungaree pocket and proceeded to dry his hands and arms.

'Glad you came,' he told them frankly. 'The farm is different this morning. Doesn't seem to be as many birds singing, or something.' He saw Jasper looking at the clean tractor. 'Well, I thought that now there would be probating of his will and maybe a sale or maybe some distant relative will show up. He wouldn't want anyone to take over the place, including the equipment, unless it was spick-and-span.'

Jasper thought that was right. 'I guess you knew him better than I thought. He had his pride, and when he was a young man he had quite a bit of it.'

Jake took them over to the porch. Conversation didn't come too easily, and Elizabeth, with mixed thoughts, partly about Rolfe, partly about Jake's own problem, was especially reticent. Even Jake noticed it, and asked a question with his quizzical eyes upon her.

'I'd like to attend the funeral with you tomorrow, if it's all right.'

She smiled. 'I was going to ask that, Jake. Do you think we ought to meet at our house in town about a half-hour early?'

He agreed. 'Sounds about right.' He looked past her at her grandfather. 'Is there an attorney in town?'

Jasper nodded, 'Old Man Foreman. John Foreman. He retired ten or twelve years ago and came back where he started from. What little legal work folks need done, he does for them.'

'Well,' said Jake, 'I'll look him up. I'll stay on until some disposition is made of everything.'

Liz picked up the implication behind that at once. 'And afterwards . . . ?'

Jake shrugged. 'I'll find a place in town, or maybe on another farm.' He looked her in the eyes. 'I won't be leaving.'

She looked out across the yard. The fields were green, some pale, some darker green. Even the fence-rows were neat and weedless. The farm looked prosperous. It seemed to reflect the pride of its late owner. In fact, it was hard, sitting there where the very strong impression of Rolfe Sumner was everywhere present, to remember that he was dead and would never again see this place where he had been born and had lived out his long life.

Jasper broke the locked-on silence that came to trouble the three people on the porch. 'Harvest time is nigh, so I expect finding another job won't be hard, Jake.'

Elizabeth looked up at Jake's strong, tanned profile, wondering things she could not ask, and in that strange, emotion-charged atmosphere she had a sudden dawning idea, a kind of strange premonition: *she was in love with this man.*

It came as a full-fledged admission. There was no doubt, no scepticism, just a gentle suggestion that came out of nowhere to fill her mind, to fill her heart and spirit, and with it came the solid conviction that usually accompanied instinctive knowledge.

It scattered her other thoughts and left her sitting there slightly limp and vulnerable. If he had turned and smiled at her, she did not know what she would do. But he kept calmly gazing straight ahead out over the sun-dazzled fields, his expression that of a man to whom death was certainly no stranger.

10

A Long Day

Old Rolfe Sumner had provided the crisis, the topic of conversation, for the year, or until something equally as momentous came to make a ripple in the placidity of village life. The gathering for his funeral was large. Some of the stores closed, less in order that their proprietors could attend than because they might as well be closed since everyone in town was out at the cemetery.

Rolfe had been a hard-headed man, and probably, as Jasper said, at one time or another, just about everyone in town had been indignant with him. But indignation rarely lasted, and this was different; this was the final tribute to someone who had gone on, and who now knew something no one else in the village knew.

Afterwards, folks filed back to their everyday lives, but the mood lingered and ruined what would otherwise have been a normal day in the village. Jake shed his tie and jacket and went out back with Elizabeth's grandfather before lunch, ostensibly to look at the garden, but she saw them through the kitchen window where she was preparing lunch, and smiled to herself, the first smile in twenty-four hours that meant anything.

They ducked into the old shed and emerged several moments later, each holding a dusty bottle of homebrew. Now, they were prepared to really wander among the vegetable rows and give her grandfather's garden their full attention.

She made a light lunch, but plenty of it. The heat was beginning to make itself noticeable; a lot of heavy food wasn't good for people in hot weather. The problem, of course, was that Jake always ate like a horse. Her interest in solving the problem between allowing him to do what probably was not good for him, and still filling him up, resolved itself into making a lot of luncheon without permitting any of it to be heavy.

Her interest in his welfare did not seem at all odd to her. After returning from the Sumner place the previous day, she'd had all afternoon to sift her feelings, and later, lying abed in the quiet darkness, to also analyse her emotions. By morning she knew the answers as well as though she'd had a mother or an aunt to go to for them.

She stood at the kitchen window watching him out there. Her grandfather, although inevitably settled a little with age, was not a short man, but Jake Bartlett loomed a head taller. Also, his movements were easy and confident, well co-ordinated, and the sun shone off his light hair and his dark-tanned skin, making him seem part of the natural environment.

She knew he was gentle and even-tempered; that he was kindly and considerate and thoughtful, but he was also a man, which meant he had a temper. She wondered what it would be like.

She stirred only when she saw them heading back towards the house, their tour of the garden completed, like their draughts of homebrew. They would stop on the way to leave the empty bottles at the shed. Her grandfather complained bitterly that since the commercial breweries had gone to those confounded twist-off beer caps, it was nigh impossible for folks to get the old-fashioned capped variety of bottle any more, so he reclaimed every bottle that was emptied.

She had set the table in the kitchen. Jake was more like one of the family than a guest; the dining-room was too large and formal anyway. She had also changed from her black dress to a gayer one, a cotton washdress, and had loosened her hair from its former severe setting. These had been natural changes for her, ones she made in the interests of comfort and ease of movement, she had not done them with any other thought in mind, but when Jake followed her grandfather into the house through the backporch, she caught the look he put upon her. It was an expression of awareness of her as a female, as a woman, of something different than a friend or a hiking companion. She could feel the electricity before Jake finished closing the backdoor, could sense his desires and needs.

It made her usual sense of poise and equilibrium shatter as though she had no defence against him. She told them to sit down while she finished serving, and kept her back to them until a measure of calm returned. But even afterwards she made a point of avoiding Jake's eyes for a while; how she felt was on her face, in her glance, as plain as a banner upon a high rampart.

It was easier, today, to talk of Rolfe.

Her grandfather said it had been a fine funeral and a good service. The minister, a youngish Anglican, had not known Rolfe. Sumner had never been a very reliable member of any congregation, like a good many people. Jasper also thought, slyly, that if Rolfe could have seen some of the mourners, such as Everette De Pugh and Jonathon Brown with whom he'd had words a time or two, Rolfe would have laughed, not at their hypocrisy for being there, but at their uneasiness in the face of something they, too, would have to face before many more summers came and went.

The heat, the standing in it at the cemetery for so long, his empty stomach, and then that potent home-brew, had all conspired quite well to make old Jasper both loud and garrulous. Jake winked at Liz and she nodded understanding, and urged her grandfather to eat his lunch.

Afterwards, the inevitable languor arrived right on schedule and Jasper excused himself to go take a nap. Jake had a little twinkle in his eye, but he said nothing until Liz said something about homebrew under a hot sun on an empty stomach. He looked across at the backwall window and grinned. 'It just comes natural to women to keep an eye on things. But you're right. And, incidentally, that's pretty darned power-ful beer he makes. The last time he gave me a bottle I had to take a nap, too.'

He helped her clear the dishes and wash them, and this time she had no objection. It was pleasant, in fact, being there like that with him. But she did not let him see her face very often as she worked at the sink. She had never before felt the ridiculous urge to blush in a man's company as often as she did with him, this afternoon. Even when he made a perfectly normal remark, she could feel the colour moving up into her cheeks.

Near the end of their labours he said, 'I was wondering, Liz . . . There's nearly a full moon this evening. Would you like to drive up atop the riverside bluff with me and see what the world looks like from up there in the moonlight?'

She held back her answer for just a fleeting moment, then said, 'All right. It ought to be cooler after sunset, too.'

He had to go back to the farm first. There were some chores that needed doing, then he would return after sundown. She went out to the front porch to see him off, and when he'd left she sat out there for a full hour, until her grandfather came padding out, yawning, thinking a lot of thoughts she'd never even considered before.

Jasper had barely sat down in a rocker nearby when she said, speaking very matter-of-factly, like a condemned person awaiting the guard, the escort to the wall, 'I'm in love with him.'

Jasper rocked a moment, then skidded the chair to a halt. He looked up, the drowsiness gone in a twinkling. 'You're what?'

'In love with Jake Bartlett,' she

repeated, in the same toneless voice.

Her grandfather sat still a moment longer, then began rocking again, the first shock past, the rationalising beginning. Man-like, old Jasper said, 'He's a hard worker and a decent young man. You'd have security with him.' That wasn't what Aggie Thorpe would have said, but right at the moment Jasper wasn't remembering anything Aggie had, or would, say. He did not know Eulalia had felt the same way. Jasper had never exchanged a confidence with Eulalia Wilson.

'Does he know?' Jasper finally asked.

She said, 'No, and I'm not going to tell him, either.'

That may, or may not, have made any sense to her grandfather, but he said, 'In time a man's bound to figure something like this out for himself. Even the ones like I was, who don't know anything about womenfolk.'

Elizabeth could have said that in time she hoped he *would* find it out, because otherwise — in time — she would have to tell him she loved him. But what she actually told her grandfather was that this was a secret they shared, and that *they alone* shared.

Jasper was agreeable. He got quiet for a long while, with the day near to ending, and finally, probably because he wanted to do some thinking by himself, he said he thought he would go out back and potter in the garden for a while. After he got down to the bottom of the stairs he looked back up, smiled at Elizabeth and winked a reassuring eye. She smiled back, and that was as near as she could come to asking his advice, and as near as he would come in giving it. From now on, the decision was entirely hers.

Later, she went indoors, to bathe and change again. It had been a day in her life that she would never forget, and it had seemed exceptionally long, exceptionally arduous.

Suppose, too, that for all the looks he gave her, for all his kindness and his tenderness towards her, Jake Bartlett was another Rolfe Sumner, another confirmed bachelor?

It was a ridiculous thought, but she had it, and she also had other thoughts equally as unseemly, like the one about Jake leaving the country. Despite what he had told her, that thought persisted while she bathed, and only dissipated afterwards when she sat at the dressing-table doing her hair.

A man named Robert Hammond, who farmed over east of town near the river, dropped by that evening to see Jasper. Elizabeth knew the Hammonds as successful and prudent farmers, people of substance who had over the generations built up a respectable stake in the community. They bought up farms, and that was what brought Hammond to see her grandfather this evening. He had, he told them, tried to contact John Foreman, the solicitor, to find out when the bidding on Sumner farm would be allowed, since old Rolfe had evidently died heirless, but Foreman hadn't been home and Hammond had thought he might be over at the Carleton place, so he'd come by.

All Elizabeth's grandfather could tell Robert Hammond was that he hadn't seen John Foreman in several days and, in any event, there was no reason for him to visit the Carletons; they had no interest in the Sumner farm.

Elizabeth had an idea where old Foreman might be: out at the farm, telling Jake what procedures were to be followed in liquidating the Sumner estate, but she did not mention this. Partly because it was too late for Hammond to drive out and make sure, and partly because she knew Robert Hammond as a typical grasping, sly Vermont Yankee, the type of New Englander even other New Englanders did not much care for.

Old Jasper elicited one interesting bit of information from Hammond. He was prepared to pay a fair market price for the Sumner farm. He had land that adjoined it, and with those two adjacencies he would be able to increase not only his land holdings, but also his farming enterprises considerably.

It was in the back of Liz's mind that perhaps Jake himself would want to bid on Sumner farm. He had mentioned wanting a farm in the vicinity. He had also said he liked the Sumner place. She tried to get Robert Hammond to say exactly how much he thought the farm was worth, and how much he would offer for it, but evidently Robert Hammond's natural shrewdness kept him from committing himself. All he would say was that it would help him widen the scope of his agricultural undertakings, and whatever he bid would have to be based on the estimated ten-year returns from such an acquisition.

That even left old Jasper, who had been a farmer and theoretically knew how farmers thought, wondering. After Robert Hammond's departure, Liz asked for an explanation. Jasper just shook his head.

'When I was young and putting in crops, we just sort of hoped there would be a decent market when we harvested, and usually there was. No one figured the sharp angles in those days. For one thing there wasn't any income tax to worry about, nor much of a land tax. All a body had to concentrate on was paying his bills and feeding his family.'

That, Liz thought, must have been a very uncomplicated time to live in, but unfortunately it did no good to think about it now, because those times were gone and unlikely to return.

A car drove up out front. She heard it because she was unconsciously listening for it. She arose, picked up her cardigan, went over to kiss old Jasper's cheek, and said, 'That's Jake. We're going for a drive this evening.' From over by the doof she also said, 'Don't wait up for me.'

Jasper nodded from his chair. He wouldn't have waited up for her anyway, at least not normally, but tonight — and he knew this instinctively — was a very special occasion in her lifetime, so perhaps tonight he would have, except that he also knew, when he reflected about it, that whatever happened tonight between his grand-daughter and Jake Bartlett, she wouldn't want to discuss it with her grandfather, and thus the meeting would be embarrassing for them both.

11

Love and the Clifftop

Elizabeth's guess had been correct; they had hardly driven away from her house when Jake said that the solicitor had been at the farm. He needed an inventory of equipment and effects, and Jake had promised to make one for him, as best he could, the following day. She offered to help, and Jake smiled.

'That was why I mentioned it. If you will write it down, I'll call it off.'

She explained about Robert Hammond, and Jake listened with interest. The only remark he made was that he would not like to see the Sumner place become just another parcel of land in someone's expanding agribusiness enterprise. Elizabeth agreed; Sumner farm was something separate and special, like a home and a personal domain.

They crossed the steel bridge and headed for the mustardy bluff without either of them acting much concerned about their destination. Jake told her he had received a letter from his parents that afternoon. He had told them of Washington, Vermont, and they wanted to see it. Probably, he told her, because he said he was thinking of settling there permanently.

She had a sudden qualm; suppose his parents arrived and did not like her, or did not like the village? Or suppose they convinced him his place was back in Nebraska, not in Vermont? She asked if they were coming to visit and he relieved her by saying that, so far, at any rate, nothing like that had been discussed.

They drove up the hill, past the lay-bys, past the old watering trough, and emerged eventually atop the bluff where moonlight made the river down below appear as a flat band of molten silver, bent out of shape as it made a curving run past the cliff.

The village was visible, too, but less as a town than as a cluster of little orange squares where windows showed lamplight among the trees and shadows.

Farther out, moonlight lay ghostly-soft upon stone fences and checkerboard fields, with here and there a lighted farmhouse. Jake looked, and left the car, to wander ahead a short distance, then he turned as Elizabeth came up, and asked why people always painted landscapes in daylight.

'This gives a different perspective, a different kind of suggestion of life down there. It shows how deep the tranquillity can become.'

She had never thought much about night-time paintings. In fact, being an eminently practical woman, she had always considered art only in the context of what was pleasing to her eyes, and a good deal that she had seen over the past few years was just the opposite. She said, 'You could do it and start a trend. Call it 'Moonlight in Vermont'.'

He smiled ruefully. 'I can't draw water. How about you?'

'The same,' she replied. 'Sorry. I'm not the arty type.'

He looked at her. 'You probably are. Have you ever experimented? I mean, sensitive people gifted with beauty have to be more than other people.'

She went slowly on over as far as the guard-chain, and stopped there with him a number of yards behind her. It would be so terribly easy, tonight, under these circumstances, to yield to him. She turned. He hadn't moved; he was looking at her steadily. She said, 'You could bid on the Sumner place, Jake. You said you liked it.'

He let his breath out slowly and strolled on up. Evidently he had hoped she wouldn't be this practical, at least right then, at that magic moment. 'I probably will,' he conceded, leaning on the big old chain. 'The part that bothers me is that if I can't finance it around here I'll have to borrow from my father to swing it, and that's no crime, of course, nor would he refuse me, but it would also give him a reason to come flying in every now and then to see that I'm farming the place right.'

She thought he was carrying his independence too far, and said so. 'Why should you work so hard at cutting yourself off, Jake? You said you loved your family; then why object if they return it by being interested in what you do?'

He hesitated before answering, as though her comment hadn't set too well with him. 'Because my father is a very domineering man, as you will see someday. And also because I'm too independent by nature, I guess.' He faced her. 'I never told them the full reason why I started wandering.'

She understood that. 'Unless you needed their opinion I don't see why you should have told them. It's your secret, Jake.'

'Yours, too,' he said, and reached to touch her hand where it lay relaxed upon one of the piers that supported the guard-chain. 'I shouldn't have made you part of my guilt, but I'll tell you an odd thing; the very next day after telling you, I began feeling better.'

She liked that. 'I'll tell you what I think, whether you want to agree with me or not. I think you've been punishing yourself for something you, as a human being, were psychologically incapable of preventing. You aren't a killer, Jake. You aren't a person who is conditioned to an impersonal attitude towards killing and towards death. You had gone your limit; even without the whisky, you were probably feeling some kind of shock, some kind of psychological reaction to horror and degradation that benumbed at least part of your mind.' She stopped speaking for a moment, then said, 'I don't know a thing about psychology, so I'm probably not making much sense.'

He called it battle fatigue. 'In the First World War they said it was shell-shock. In the Second War it was called battle fatigue, or combat trauma.

And at least you are right about the numbness. I was already feeling that when I found the bottle of whisky among the medical supplies. It would make you sick to hear some of the things I saw during that Red offensive.'

'Jake, did you see other men do things that upset you?'

He made a squirting little brittle laugh. 'God, yes, by the dozen.'

'Did you condemn them for it?'

'No, you can't judge people under those circumstances.'

She had made her point perfectly. 'But that's exactly the issue, Jake: you don't believe in punishing them, but you have been punishing yourself ever since, and you were no different.'

He stood in silence for a while, then turned slightly, twisting from the waist, to look down across the river towards the village. 'I was supposed to know better. I was trained.'

She hammered at him, hard. 'Jake, you were a man of feeling, of sensitivity, in a place where terrible things were happening. You were doing your duty and it was turning you inside out. You were trained for something different than blood in the mud and jungle, and wholesale murder. Everyone has a point beyond which they cannot go. You found yours that night, or day, whichever it was. It wasn't dereliction and it certainly wasn't cowardice, it was simply a limit, a rejection of horror.'

He let her get it all said, and kept looking down across the peaceful world of Vermont, serene in moonlight with its forest-hills dark against a pale horizon, against a pale-vaulted heaven where the moon rode its ancient course, crossing from mountain to mountain, and lighting up all the intersecting valleys.

He turned towards her. 'I get so damned tired of thinking about it, sometimes,' he said, allowing a long interval of silence to run out before speaking again. 'You're right, I reached my limit after thirty-six hours. I wasn't afraid. Hell, I'd been on the line with the combat people for seven hours, burning ammunition against those human assault waves; it was such a terrible waste, the way they'd send them in trying to over-run us with sheer numbers. Then I went back to my medic job when the assaults weakened. We'd taken a lot of casualties, too. They said the disparity was seven-to-one, and maybe it was, but the rows of wounded I had to go back to looked awfully long to me. Some died before the medics could get to them. It was a nightmare. It began raining . . . ' He let out a long, unsteady breath. 'Anyway, you are right, I went up as far as I could go, and *that* was where I failed.'

'You didn't fail,' she averred. 'You shouldn't have been left like that for so long. No one could stand it for thirty-six hours.'

He gazed steadily at her as he said, 'Liz, you're the best thing that's happened to me in my entire lifetime, but particularly since — then.'

She had thought something would happen between them tonight; had thought that at least something *might* happen between them, tonight, providing he had any of the feelings for her she had for him, and she had schooled herself to handle it calmly, but after their impassioned discussion, with her emotions aroused in his defence, with her breath coming hard, she was off-balance when it began to seem that the personal aspect had arrived. She thought of a defence, but he did not give her much chance to raise it.

'You're the only person I've ever told that story to, who has made it seem even remotely justified in the only way it can be justified. And you're a girl.'

He said that last sentence as though he were surprised that reason could come from a woman. She would ordinarily have said something about that, but not tonight, because she was listening, not speaking.

'You've taken most of the pain out of it, Liz, most of the reason for the bad dreams. But it still doesn't leave me looking heroic, does it? I mean, I stood it for as long as most of them, but in the end I reached a limit, too.'

She wanted him to go on talking, to get it all out into the open, but he only spoke in fits and starts, as though this were the way he had to purge himself, and eventually, as their emotionalism diminished, he left that subject almost entirely.

'I'll tell you, Liz, that whatever else I am, it's not a man-killer, it's not a soldier. But the hell of it is that most men think they are capable, and many are, but just not everyone. I thank God I'll never have to do it again.' He raised an arm and pointed. 'There's the church spire with the cross atop it. Can you see that?'

She turned to look, and when she did so, his arm fell and his hand touched her shoulder, turning her very gently. She came around easily and went into his arms with two short forward steps. His mouth sought her lips, which were lifted to him, and he struggled with himself, she could feel it in him, feel him holding back. She didn't want that, she wanted him. She raised both arms to encircle his shoulders, to press as close as she could get, and that made his ardour slip its leash.

He slid his hot face alongside her cheek. She waited, expecting him to speak, but he remained silent. His body was tense, so she turned soft and yielding against him to winnow away the tightness, and succeeded. He loosened against her.

Finally, she eased back, unafraid to meet his gaze, reached to run bent fingers through his hair, and wonder at the searing fire she had emanated because she had always thought the initiative in such a moment as this belonged to the man, and yet she had met his fire with one to equal it. Evidently she didn't know herself as well as she thought.

He straightened up, after a bit, holding her hands, standing back and smiling at her with a kind of moon-lighted wistfulness. 'I couldn't leave here if I had to,' he said quietly. 'I knew that the first time we were together hiking up that darned mountainside.'

Her heart was beating solidly as she said, 'Knew what?'

'I was in love with you, Liz, like I've never been able to even think of loving another woman.'

She leaned against him, burrowing into his chest with her face. She wanted to cry, but that would only spoil things, so she fought that down and clung to him until the spasms had passed. She did not tell him that she, too, was in love. She didn't say anything at all while he held her and talked softly in the moonlight.

'It's the things a man thinks about, sometimes, that don't seem to have any basis in reality, that influence his life. I was standing there listening to that preacher at the funeral, and thinking that some way, somehow, I had to find a way to ask you to marry me. It wasn't the right place to think of it, but the urge was overpowering, like I was being made to think like that. And at luncheon, later, whenever I looked at you, Liz, I thought of that.'

She remembered how he had looked at her, and how she had instinctively known some of his thoughts; she had been unnerved by them and had avoided his eyes throughout luncheon.

'If anything happens, Liz . . . I mean, if it doesn't work out, I'll never feel this way towards a girl again. I know that, because I know it's just not possible to ever feel this way but once in your life.'

She reared back and lifted her face with the starshine reflecting in her eyes. 'Why shouldn't it work out, Jake?' She raised both arms to the back of his neck and brought his head down gently until their lips met. Then, gentle though her hands were, the passion surged up again in them both.

For Liz it was like a gigantic explosion that did not make a sound. Her entire being responded to his nearness, to the hungers she felt in him, and to the pressure of his lips, as though this were her sole purpose for being.

Finally, when she could turn her face and free herself a little, she said, 'I love you, Jake. I didn't realise it as early as you did, but I knew what it was that day out at the Sumner place when we were sitting on the porch, and I was watching you.'

12

Love is a New World

Liz was tardy arising the next morning. While she was dressing she smelled the coffee and the bacon, which meant that her grandfather, arising at his usual hour, and hungry as he invariably was in the morning, had given up waiting for her.

She did not hurry, not this morning. She wasn't quite up to walking out into the kitchen and greeting her grandfather with a hypocritical airiness as though nothing had happened between her and Jake last night, that kept her out until the small hours.

Later, after her grandfather had hiked out to the garden in order to do whatever strenuous work had to be done before the heat arrived, Liz went out and made herself a piece of toast and a cup of tea. She sat and remembered, and wasn't aware of the time until the telephone rang and it was Jake wanting to know if she had forgotten that she'd volunteered to help him make the physical inventory this morning. She promised to be right out, put down the telephone and ran out back to ask her grandfather if she could use his car.

Jasper leaned on a hoe-handle and watched her hasten up. 'Where's the fire?' he asked, and smiled.

'I promised Jake I'd help him take inventory this morning. He just called to ask when I'd be out. Do you mind if I use the car?'

Jasper shook his head. 'Don't mind at all. Was John Foreman at the farm last night when Bob Hammond was looking for him?'

She said, 'Yes,' and kissed his leathery old cheek, then turned and ran to the garage. Jasper continued to lean and watch her, and as the car sputtered to life he confided in the hoe-handle that he wouldn't want to be her age again, and have to go through all she was about to go through, again, for all the tea in China. Then he went back to work, stirring the topsoil, and as the heat built up, edging his way closer and closer to the old shed.

For Elizabeth, the trip through town northward reminded her that she'd left a grocery list atop the kitchen table, and that she would have to stop at Brown's general store on her way back if she and her grandfather were to have a decent supper tonight. Otherwise, she cruised on through and made the three-mile run to the gate of Sumner farm in very good time.

Jake had fitted out a clipboard with some lined sheets of paper. He greeted her with a peck on the cheek, then handed over a pencil and the clipboard without showing anything in his expression while he explained to her how he thought they ought to make their inventory.

'Leave the house until the last, and

start out here at the equipment shed, working our way around through the barn and outbuildings. What do you think of that?'

What she thought was that, after what they had been to each other the previous night, he should have greeted her with a much more passionate and prolonged kiss. But what she said was: 'I don't know a single thing about farm machinery, Jake.'

He stood gazing at her, his mind obviously wandering. Then he jerked himself back to the present and said, 'Don't worry, I'll name the stuff.' He took her arm and led her over to the doorway of the equipment shed. They both stopped there, cowed. There were tools over, on, and beneath all three workbenches. There was an accumulation of at least one generation, and probably two generations, that would have made the most hardened inventory-taker pause.

He said, 'Hell's bells, if we list every individual tool in here we'll be working in just the shed for another day or two.'

'How about 'Sundry hand tools'?' she asked. 'Or 'Sundry small hand tools'?'

He liked that, so that was their first entry. He liked the idea so well he kissed her cheek, and she left the letter 'd' out of sundry and had to erase and begin over.

There were two tractors, a high-wheeled seed drill, a baler, two springtooth cultivators, both very old, a three-bottom plough, and an endless variety of other tractor-attachments, such as a mulcher, that Liz had never heard of before. There was a stone-boat, but she was familiar with that because anyone living in New England knew how picking up stones from the fields was part of the farming scene.

She filled four pages with close-spaced entries, and that was before they had finished outside. Jake leaned over her shoulder to read the last page, and nuzzled her neck, which made her loosen her grip on the clipboard. He said, 'I knew right from the beginning we'd make a terrific team.'

She edged away. Not that she objected to the little shows of affection, but standing in the centre of a farmyard was not her idea of the logical place to demonstrate them.

He seemed to realise this, and as they were finishing up outside he teased her by slipping an arm round her waist, by occasionally leaning so close it was practically impossible for her to write, by telling her how lovely she was and otherwise distracting her. She did not get exasperated, although with someone else she would have. He was making up for what she had thought had not been an adequately amorous reception when she first arrived.

Finally, they entered the old house. She had been inside it before, but remembered nothing very clearly. One old-fashioned parlour in Vermont was pretty much like all the others.

There were a number of Sumners hanging on the walls of both the parlour and the dining-room. Some of the furniture looked as though it belonged to those older Sumners. There was an exquisite little rosewood writing desk that did not match anything else in the parlour, and which it was easy to imagine some long-departed Sumner woman polishing and dusting with tender care.

There was a good bit of old-fashioned pewter, pitchers, mugs, serving dishes, odds and ends like salt-shakers and candle-snuffers that Elizabeth recognised but which Jake had trouble putting a name to. Candle-snuffers especially and things like that.

The dining-room was Elizabeth's domain. She made her own inventory and when she was finished she missed Jake, so she wandered elsewhere, into a sewing-room so thick with dust it was hard to imagine anyone even opening the door in the past fifty years, and from there she went out to the pantry to continue with her work, and only missed her partner when she encountered a series of copper coils, laden with dust, hooked up to a wooden barrel, with a small stove evidently vented out through the cellar, connected with the barrel. She *thought* the contraption was a whisky-still. Her grandfather would have known at once, and she was certain Jake would be able to identify the thing, but when she retraced her steps he was not in the front of the house at all.

She found him out front on the porch, talking to a man whom she recognised even though his back was to her as she looked out a front window: Robert Hammond.

She leaned to look for his car, found it out beyond the picket-gate, and wondered that she hadn't heard him drive up. She considered going out, then decided not to. Jake's wide shoulders were to the front door, effectively barring it. She would have to disturb him to go out, and evidently he had taken that position to bar access to Hammond.

She heard Hammond say: 'Well, I can see a copy of the inventory at Foreman's office anyway. It would just save a little time if I knew what equipment there was. I might not want any of it, anyway. Probably all old stuff, eh?'

Jake's answer was smooth. 'All you've had to do for several years, Mister Hammond, was look over the fence to see what equipment he had. And you're perfectly correct, you can see the inventory when we're through with it, at Mister Foreman's office.'

'We?' said Hammond. 'You have help making this inventory?'

Evidently that struck Jake wrong because he said, 'Look, you've said what you came to say, and I've answered it. Now what else do you want around here — before you leave?'

Liz saw burly Bob Hammond's shoulders square up, saw his back stiffen. 'Some civil answers from a common hired hand,' he rapped right back, and glared.

Jake did not flinch. 'You got them. Is there anything else?'

Bob Hammond was angry. Liz, who knew him passably well, saw the splotchy colour mount, saw the way his jaw was set when he turned profile to her. Without another word he slammed down off the porch and out to his car. This time she heard the engine when he backed clear, shifted gears and went furiously out of the yard. She stepped to the door, opened it and slid out to stand beside Jake watching the car stir clouds of dust as it sped away.

'Now you've met Bob Hammond,' she told Jake. 'The man of whom it is said no one can equal him in sharp land deals and few are his equals as farmers. You made him mad.'

Jake was not very concerned. 'He's probably been angry before. Anyway, he was too darned nosy for my taste.' He looked at her pensive expression, smiled and encircled her neck from the back with one hand, tipped up her face and kissed her on the lips. Then he said it was lunchtime and he had a cold ham roast in the oven they could warm up.

They forgot about Bob Hammond, at least for the balance of that day. She handed him the clipboard, made him sit in a kitchen chair while she made their luncheon, and, when he was impressed at how well she had inventoried the rooms she had visited while he'd been out on the porch, she told him of the weird contraption with the copper tubing, and he burst out laughing.

'It's a whisky still. Rolfe showed it to me one day when he was poking fun at his forefathers. They used to make a brand of old pop-skull, he said, that would take the varnish off a bar-room table.'

She pointed to the clipboard. 'Write it down. One whisky still, complete but old.'

He sat a moment, pencil poised, then shrugged and wrote it exactly as she had worded it.

She had not gone down into the cellar. He said they would do that together after lunch. Also, there were three bedrooms upstairs that probably hadn't had anyone sleep in them in almost a hundred years, but they were furnished, so they would also have to be inventoried.

She said nothing about it, but the kitchen of the Sumner place, while spotless, had no fresh vegetables in any of the bins, and one cupboard was full to the ceiling with every imaginable variety of tinned mixtures such as vegetables and lamb, beans with pork, cod with boiled potatoes, and beef with noodles. She could imagine the two of them, Jake and old Rolfe Sumner, making a sloppy supper each night and eating heartily of some of these concoctions because they were hungry, and for no other reason, but she marvelled that they had neither of them evidently thought what an unhealthy way that was to eat. She made up her mind that in the future she would look after Jake's diet because, very obviously, he wouldn't do it.

After lunch they inventoried the cellar, where mash barrels, among other forgotten old treasures, stood in gloomy mustiness, and where Liz felt decidedly uneasy because there were mouseholes all along the old oiled floor. Then they went upstairs to inventory the three bedrooms, and found a hush, a musty silence that was eerie to say the least.

One of the bedrooms had a woman's clothing hanging in a wardrobe. To Jake this meant nothing. To Liz, who knew the styles, this had to have been Rolfe Sumner's mother's room. Nothing in that wardrobe was newer than the year 1900.

They finished the inventory and stood in the vestibule at the head of the stairs, looking over what had been written down. He thought they might have listed a lot of odds and ends that Mister Foreman didn't actually want. She insisted that an inventory was supposed to include everything. He smiled, nuzzled her cheek, and when she winced, he took the clipboard from her, balanced it atop a post at the head of the stairway, took her in his arms with a strength that left her slightly breathless, and kissed her without a single inhibition.

She felt her passions flaring, placed both hands against his chest, and pushed clear. 'It's not good for you to get excited on a full stomach,' she said, and they both laughed. He did not loosen his grip very much, though, even though she squirmed.

He said, 'Liz . . . will you marry me?'

She didn't hesitate. 'Yes. But when?'

His eyes twinkled. 'How about this afternoon?'

She finally broke free and caught her breath from the effort. 'You know that's impossible. But maybe, if we didn't plan too elaborate a wedding, it could take place next week . . . Except . . . '

'Yes, except what?'

'Your parents, Jake.'

'But they're not marrying you, I am.'

She was adamant. 'No, Jake. I wouldn't want a son of mine to treat me like that. You can't do that to your mother. I won't let you.'

He relented. 'All right. I'll telephone them tonight that we're to be married next week, and I'll let them know the exact day later. How is that?'

She went into his arms again. For her, this being in love was such a totally new and different world.

13

A Lover's Reflections

There were disadvantages to being in love; for example, although she had known she should stop at the grocery store on her way home late that afternoon, she cruised past and didn't even think of marketing until she walked into the kitchen at home and saw her grocery list.

She was spared having to make-do, however, because Mister Brown did not close until six o'clock. She snatched up the list and made a hurried run back into the centre of town.

Evidently she was not the only late shopper. She met Agatha Thorpe at the baked-goods counter, and near the meat counter she saw Eulalia Wilson. She avoided Agatha, but spoke briefly with Eulalia, otherwise her shopping expedition was successful without being very exciting.

Back home, she went in search of her grandfather, and found him napping out back in the shade of a giant beech tree. She did not have to be told his drowsiness was the result of at least two trips to the toolshed this afternoon, because she could smell the homebrew on him.

She returned to the house to get dinner, and the telephone rang. It was Jake with a suggestion that he take her to dinner tonight. She had already begun supper so she reneged, but she invited him to come eat with them, and he wouldn't do that because it was beginning to look as though he were going to establish a permanent residence at the Carleton place. But he did promise to see her the next day.

She went back to her work, smiling. When her grandfather finally came in, hungry and rumpled, she sent him to wash up first, then set their meal upon the table, and when he returned she told him of her adventures as an inventory-taker.

Jasper remembered the pictures on the walls at the Sumner place, and, in fact, he remembered Rolfe's parents very well. The others he was less certain about. When Liz mentioned the still, old Jasper had a fit of laughter.

'During Prohibition, in the 'twenties, when the only way a man could get a nip was to manufacture it himself, stills were fairly common. But mostly, folks cooked their booze with firewood, and that was how the Sumners got caught. I recollect that as well as though it were yesterday. Folks don't very often have smoke coming out of their chimneys in July and August. Some revenue agents saw that, as they were driving through our community, and got a warrant, then went back and made their search. It caused quite a scandal. Of course, everyone else was doing the same thing, but it was customary for folks to be scandalised. That way, they figured, the revenue men wouldn't come down on them.'

The telephone rang again. Liz went to answer it. This time the caller was John Foreman and he wanted to speak to Jasper. Liz went back, told her grandfather he was wanted out in the hall where the telephone was, and resumed her dinner. It did not occur to her to be interested in the telephone call, but when her grandfather returned, she got interested.

Jasper sat back down, then said, 'What happened between Jake and Bob Hammond? Bob's all fired up to buy the Sumner place and throw Jake off.'

Liz told him about the brief disagreement on the porch. Jasper mulled that over and came to the conclusion that it had to be more than that; he had known Bob Hammond as a boy and a man for a good many years, and while he was willing to concede that Hammond was a little vindictive, and at times downright pig-headed, he was not the kind of man who would risk a single penny for revenge.

'If he wants Jake off, up there, you can bet your money it's for some other reason than just plain revenge.'

They discussed this for a while, but since neither could come up with a reason for Hammond to be so assertive, except the obvious one which Jasper had ruled out, they dropped the topic and turned to something much closer to home: Jake's proposal of marriage, and Elizabeth's acceptance of it.

Old Jasper liked Jake very much, but he was nonetheless cautious. 'Suppose you waited until next spring,' he said. 'It never does any harm to make right sure about those things. I could tell you of a round dozen folks right here in Washington hastened into marriage and repented at their leisure.'

Liz smiled across the table. 'We're going to wait. We decided to do nothing, until next week.'

Jasper blinked. 'Married — next week?'

Elizabeth reached to pat his hand. 'Trust us,' she said. 'Have faith in our judgement. I can tell you this much: if I waited until next spring it wouldn't change anything. I love him, he loves me. We want to be married.'

Jasper sighed and finished his supper without saying much more. He was just beginning to have the terrible doubts that the male protector of every young female has when he sees her slipping away, pulled from him by a younger man with a powerful mating instinct. It did not matter that he was her grandfather instead of her father; as far as he was concerned she had no other guardian.

He had worked very hard for many years to bring her up to this point. It had not been easy, except the last year or so. He went out into the parlour and switched on some lamps, then sat in his chair opposite the television set, stared at the blank tube and did not switch the thing on.

What might come of this love-match? What could come of *any* love match? Probably the chances were fifty-fifty, success or failure. It was the dark side that frightened him now, the uncertainty, and the tribulation of love itself. He knew from dim memory that love was nothing simple, even though it seemed so at first.

The gloominess that had settled, bowed him down and rode his spirit, until Elizabeth came into the parlour smelling of hand lotion after doing the dishes, looked at his face, looked at the blank television tube, and went to switch the set on for him as she said, 'Are you brooding about the marriage? Believe me, Grandfather, there will never be another man like him, where I'm concerned, so even if I were making a mistake, which I know I'm not, I'd still have to marry him. Does that kind of a feeling for someone mean anything at all?'

He nodded, satisfied she was in love with young Jake Bartlett, but, as he knew, love was only the first part of lifelong mating. In fact, after something like thirty years, it wasn't the same kind of feeling at all. The flames were banked, the coals were cooling. Then, living with the same woman was different; a man did not feel any the less for her, but he felt *differently*.

But, thirty years ahead was a very long while, considering they wouldn't even be married until next week. Old Jasper straightened up with an effort, took down a big, ragged breath and let it out noisily. 'All I want for you is happiness,' he said. 'But I guess happiness is different things at different times. I want you both to be healthy — and you'll know how important that is someday. The happiness, well, you'll find out eventually that you have to make that for yourselves.'

She went to affectionately kiss him, then she sat on the sofa feeling settled and mature, feeling every inch a woman. Even the memory of girlhood couldn't intrude at this time. 'Whatever happens to him, Grandfather, will have to happen to us both, the good and the bad. I want it that way. I welcome it, even the bad. What good is a woman to a man if she isn't more than simply a lover to him?'

Old Jasper blushed, but it went unnoticed in the parlour light. 'Don't be too eager,' he said dryly, 'there will be bad. If you live long enough you'll see your share of the bad in life; there just doesn't seem to be any way to get around that. It's a test for couples, all right, and a good many don't pull through it still together.'

She had no doubts at all. 'We will.'

Jasper let his gaze drift to the television screen, where *café au lait* people with great mops of unclean-looking fuzzy hair were screaming out some Afric kind of song. He grimaced and went over to switch channels. He kept switching until he found a cowboy drama, then retreated to his chair in comfort. He had not said everything in his mind about Elizabeth's love and her marriage, but at least for the time being he had.

She sat complacently and also

watched television, but deep down she was restless. After a while she went out front and stood by an upright porch-post watching the moon soar in a streaked sky. It was going to rain, but she did not notice that. The ribbons of darkness stretching overhead meant something different to her; they signi-fied the storminess of mated life. Perhaps her mood had been influenced by her grandfather's attitude.

She felt compelled to face her thoughts of the future defensively, something she had never done before. If someone had explained that love called forth every emotion in a woman not once but dozens of times during her first travails, Liz would have understood why she felt this way now. But there was no one to tell her; as always, she had to rely upon herself for every explanation, now that she was a woman.

The village was lighted around her, treetops stood dark against the night, and flower-fragrance, like the summer-time smells of daytime, were everywhere. There wasn't a breath of wind, but then wind usually, at least in mid-year, did not trouble mountainous New England.

A dog barked somewhere, up closer to the centre of town, and a car-horn honked impatiently. It wasn't bed-time yet, so the village had its little homely sounds. Up at the farm the loudest noise would be a barn-owl hooting or perhaps a vixen-fox yapping somewhere along a stone fence where she did her nocturnal mouse-hunting.

She wondered if Jake had called his parents. She even tried to anticipate a mother's reaction when her youngest son said he was going to take a wife. Pain, she thought, pain and a quick-rushing sensation of sadness would come over the woman. The sadness would be only in part because she was losing a child, she thought; it would also mean that the mother was nearing an end to her usefulness. It was hard to imagine life without being needed.

Inside, the telephone rang. Elizabeth,

far off in sombre thought, gave a little start. Then her grandfather came and looked out into the shadows.

'Liz? It's for you. It's Jake.'

She hastened inside with a quickening heart-beat. Her grandfather went back to the parlour, although actually it was his bedtime. He had another cowboy movie on the television set and seemed too engrossed in the plot to realise he was breaking one of his own rules.

Jake hadn't called for any particular reason, he told her, except that he'd been sitting out front on the porch and he kept having a strong urge to call her, as though she were wishing he would. She laughed, but did not tell him she had also been outside with her thoughts.

She asked if he had called his parents. He had. 'About an hour ago. I spoke to my father first. He seemed pleased. My mother sniffled a little. I guess having her baby marry is harder on her than on anyone else. They want to fly up. I told them I'd write the details of the wedding, and for them to wait until they heard from us before coming.'

Elizabeth didn't like that. 'Why? Why didn't you tell them to come right away?'

'You don't mind?'

'Mind?' she answered. 'I'm scairt stiff, but it's got to be done. Did you know there is a landing strip east of town a mile or two? It's kept up by the government as an emergency landing field. If we know what day they'll arrive we can be out there to meet them.'

Jake submitted. 'All right. I'll get off a letter to them first thing in the morning, and that will be settled. They'll love you. Not as much as I do, and in a different way, but they'll love you nonetheless.'

Liz let some of her trepidation show by saying, 'I certainly hope so, Jake.' Then, to cover up, she asked if she would see him the next day. He laughed about that.

'You couldn't keep me away if you filled the yard with lions. I'm going to take our inventory list to Mister Foreman before noon, then I'll be over.'

When he mentioned the solicitor it put her in mind of Bob Hammond; she wondered if he had heard any more from Hammond. He hadn't, and he was of the opinion that he wouldn't, at least not directly, after their little dispute on the porch.

He seemed perfectly willing to forget the Hammond matter. She felt differently, but then she knew some of the tales that were abroad concerning Hammond, and Jake had probably never heard them.

She kept her forebodings to herself; plenty of time to tell him if something cropped up. Moreover, she could very possibly be letting her imagination run away with her; very possibly Bob Hammond had decided not to press his dislike of Jake Bartlett.

They talked a little longer, not about anything important but just in order to be talking to one another, then Liz said her grandfather had just marched past on his way to bed, the last cowboy movie having ended, and she thought it might be a good idea if they also retired.

Jake said, 'I love you. Sleep well and dream of us together.'

She smiled unconsciously. 'I do that anyway. Good night, Jake.'

14

A Casual Fortune

Elizabeth's premonition was more correct than even she gave it credit for being. When Jake arrived the following day slightly after ten o'clock, he had a little bombshell to drop. Jasper had walked over to a friend's place, another retired farmer who had a garden patch, so he wasn't there to hear it.

'Hammond has had the Sumner place appraised on his own, and he has made a tentative offer — in cash — to John Foreman. There are two stipulations: one is that he be allowed to move in right away, within the next month or less, to start preparing the ground for an early seeding next spring, and the other stipulation is that Foreman gives me notice and gets me off the place within the same length of time — within a month or less.'

Elizabeth was upset. She was also indignant. 'I'd like to give him a piece of my mind,' she exclaimed, and did not smile back when Jake laughed at her. 'It's serious, Jake. Anyone around the village can tell you that when Bob Hammond goes after something, he usually gets it.'

'Mister Foreman told me that when we were looking over the inventory,' Jake related. 'He doesn't like being in the middle, and he doesn't like being held up by the court.'

Liz, who knew nothing of probating, said, 'What court?'

'The one over at Edgerton, the county seat, the local superior court that Mister Foreman sent a petition to allowing him to open Rolfe Sumner's bank deposit box, and to go through the papers in the desk out at the farm. Before anything can be done at all, according to Foreman, it has to be proved that Rolfe Sumner died intestate, died without a will and without heirs.'

Liz had heard her grandfather say a dozen times that Rolfe was the last of the Sumners, that he didn't even have any distant relations. But when she mentioned that, Jake was of the opinion that it made no difference; what the law demanded was proof one way or another.

'And meanwhile,' she said gloomily, 'can John Foreman lease the place to Bob Hammond?'

Jake shook his head. 'No; he's got to find the disposition Rolfe Sumner wanted made of the estate. If he can't do that, if there was no will and last testament, as Foreman suspects, on the basis that a lot of those old-timers don't make wills, then the estate will be administered by the court until such time as a final disposition can be made of it. That means until the farm is declared the property of the State of Vermont. Then it can be sold to the highest bidder.'

She said, 'Bob Hammond,' as though it were a foul word.

Jake smiled. 'Don't give up. That brings up something else: would you want to live out there, after we're married?'

She looked up at him. 'At the Sumner farm?'

'Yes. Because if you want to, Bob Hammond is going to find himself with a strong competitor for the farm. Me.'

She *had* thought of them living *somewhere*, but only in a vague and dream-like way. Now, she had to buckle down to a single specific thought, and that was rushing things a little. Still, she did love the countryside, and she had always admired the old Sumner place. There was a large yard out back. The fence needed mending, but at one time it had been an ideal place for small children to be penned in.

She blushed and crossed the parlour to stand at a back window, gazing out, her back to Jake. 'I love the place,' she told him. 'It's what you want, isn't it?'

He walked over, turned her and held her at arm's length. 'What I want is you — and whatever will make you happy.'

She pushed forward and put her cheek against his chest. 'Sumner farm,' she murmured, and that seemed to settle it. He kept both arms locked round her as he agreed that they would fight for the farm.

She remembered what he'd said about not wanting to borrow money from his parents. Washington had a branch-bank, but her grandfather had said a hundred times that to borrow enough money to do anything except pay an overdue grocery bill was impossible.

She snuggled closer and said, 'The money, Jake.'

He understood her thinking. 'My folks, if necessary, but I'll try other sources first.'

'Not the local bank, Jake, because grandfather says it never loans enough for anything that ambitious.'

He let his breath out as though her

remark had burst a balloon for him. 'There will be other sources,' he said, without sounding very hopeful, and his grip on her loosened, so she leaned back to look up at him.

'If your parents can do it, and if they want to do it, why not let them?'

'I told you why,' he responded.

She did not yield. 'Jake, if you have an understanding with your father right from the outset — this is *your* farm and *your* life, and he's welcome only by invitation, wouldn't that make him realise you are a man now, an *independent* man, just like he is?'

Jake released her, all but one hand, and with that he took her back to the sofa and sat her down at his side. 'Wait until you've met my father,' he told her, crookedly smiling. 'He's wealthy and successful, and he knows farming and the money markets backwards and forwards. He's dynamic and makes Robert Hammond look like an amateur when it comes to steamrollering his way through life. I think it was the similarity

I recognised in Hammond on the porch yesterday that angered me. Otherwise, since I didn't know the man, I can't imagine why I should have reacted that way to his overbearing attitude.'

It was getting close to lunch time. She didn't ask if he was hungry; she simply took him out to the kitchen with her, sat him at the table and went to work over his protests, and made luncheon for them both. There was plenty if her grandfather returned in time to eat, but she knew how that went; when two old men got together in the shade somewhere, they would reminisce, talk, argue, discuss everything from politics to crops, and wouldn't either one of them remember that it was time to eat.

He told her he had tried to get some clue from John Foreman about what the Sumner farm would sell for. Foreman had acted irritable. 'He said he had retired from the practice of law once, and he didn't like being pulled back into a case that could end up in a superior court hearing, if Hammond kept pushing, and if I kept acting like I was going to be troublesome.'

She understood. 'John Foreman is as old as my grandfather. He's comfortably well off. He grew up here, and when he retired from practising law down in New York, he came back here. He specialises in drawing up wills, in representing merchants against overdue accounts, that sort of thing.'

Jake made a face. 'If a man works at his profession at all, sweetheart, then he should expect to have to *work* at it, at least occasionally. Where is there another lawyer?'

She said there would be some over at the capitol, or at Edgerton, but she knew nothing about any of them. She smiled at that kind of ignorance. 'We don't have lawsuits around Washington.'

He grinned back as she set a heaping plate of cold cuts before him. 'I'll get a reputation for being a trouble-maker.'

She doubted it. 'Not as long as you

fight people like Bob Hammond. He couldn't win a popularity contest around here.' She filled a glass with chilled tea for him, sat opposite him at the table with a very modest plateful, and shook her head at the way he ate. 'If you ever stop being very active, Jake, and keep your present appetite, you are going to be as big as a house.'

He winked. 'I don't know how to sit back and drowse in a rocking-chair. Maybe in the springtime you could help me plant the oats. That would keep you in pretty good shape, too.'

She said, 'No, thanks. I'll try to stay in shape without becoming a fieldhand. I remember when I was a little girl, seeing some of the farm women ride to town with their husbands in the summertime — red-handed, turkey-necked, tanned in the face and wrinkled as prunes. My grandfather used to say New England is a wonderful country for men, but hell on horses and women.'

They laughed together, and afterwards he kept looking at her with a twinkle in his eye. 'You're the only person I can be around when I'm brooding, and the mood just evaporates. You can bring a smile just by standing in one place. No other woman has ever been able to do that with me.'

Her response was as dry as old corn husks. 'How many other women have you given the opportunity to do that with you?'

'My mother and my aunt, in Nebraska, and a girl I met one time in Kansas City before I went overseas.'

Her blue eyes were cynical. 'And one or two others in Oregon, at the University, and another few here and there. Jake, you're a good-looking man. Don't deceive me — just don't ever give another one a chance.'

Jasper came barging in from out back. He saw Jake and boomed a hearty greeting as he paused on the rear porch to wash his hands at the laundry tub. 'Hot enough out,' he called, 'to bring on the second tomato crop in ten days. But it's going to rain, maybe tonight, and that's welcome, too.'

Jasper combed his thin hair, showed Elizabeth his clean hands, and as she got up to fix his plate he drew out a chair, sat loosely, and sighed. 'It's the danged humidity. Just before a rain a man could stand in the shade and wring himself out a quart of perspiration without even breathing hard.'

Liz frowned and her grandfather saw it. Odd thing about womenfolk, what was a basic, commonplace fact of everyday living, if it got mentioned at the dining-table, it was crude and unmannerly. Jasper shrugged, leaned back and said, 'The rumour is round town that you and Bob Hammond are going to lock antlers over the Sumner place.'

Jake thought that was a pretty accurate rumour. 'It could come to that, I guess.'

Jasper leaned back for Elizabeth to put the plate in front of him, and in the most casual of tones, said, 'Well, if you need financing, I could probably help out.'

Both the younger people stopped and stared. It had never crossed Elizabeth's mind that her grandfather would be a source of money. In fact, it had never crossed her mind that he might have anything beyond the expense-money he put out each month for the household expenses, and which came in part from a World War One pension, and in part from an old-age allotment.

Jake raised his eyes to Elizabeth. She didn't know what to say; it crossed her mind that her grandfather had made that magnanimous offer without really appreciating how values had skyrocketed since he'd been a farmer many years earlier; very possibly old Jasper was thinking in terms of land values in the 1920s or 1930s.

As she sat down she said, 'The farm has to be properly appraised first, Grandad, and it will be an inflated value because everything else is inflated nowadays.'

Jasper nodded and began eating his lunch. 'Yup. It's a darned shame that those tax-people are allowed to break farmers just because no one really understands how much land it takes in Vermont, with our short season, for a man to make a living off the land. I suppose they'll put the Sumner place up around maybe fifty or sixty thousand dollars, eh?'

Elizabeth was too stunned to answer. It was inconceivable to her that her grandfather, who had been driving the same car for eleven years, had that kind of money. Inconceivable and downright unbelievable.

Across from her, Jake was mentioning that his parents would probably be willing to finance Sumner farm. Jasper listened to that, while he ate, and afterwards he offered an opinion that was a lot closer to home than he could possibly have known.

'Well, Jake, sometimes borrowing

from a man's folks isn't very wise. Come a few bad years and you miss some payments, and it causes anguish on both sides.'

Jake said, 'But you're folks, too,' and old Jasper came back with another bombshell answer.

'It's different with me, Jake. I'm not going to loan you the money. I'm going to give it to the pair of you. It would go to Liz anyway, as soon as I died, and just because I won't be doing that for awhile isn't any reason to keep it in the bank when Sumner farm is at stake.'

Elizabeth was dumbfounded. So was Jake. Old Jasper went right on with his lunch as though what they had been discussing had more to do with the approaching promise of rain than with a fortune casually offered. In fact, Jasper went further; he began discussing the garden his friend had, and where he had spent the morning. He may have been doing that to permit the astonished younger people to recover, and he may have been doing it because he was seriously more interested in that topic than in wealth; a man his age, with his background and principles, was just as likely to be more interested in what the ground would yield, than in money.

It was a fact that old farmers, old men of any kind of rural background, appeared to view money with less and less fascination as they advanced in years. They probably had made the basic discovery that people whose sole interest in life was money were the most lonely of all people, and usually this happened even before they were old.

15

A Surprise Message

It rained that night, hard, but because the earth was warm, and the stillness and the midsummer heat remained, even at night, the rain did not bring much coolness with it.

New England, like Old England, was a place that had little use for the varieties of artificial watering — called irrigation — that had to be employed in more arid lands. On the other hand, the people who farmed in those wetter places rarely were able to put up a dry hay crop.

As Jake said the next morning when Jasper and his grand-daughter drove out to Sumner farm and found him at the equipment shed readying a hayrake, 'If you don't put it in the barn it'll lie out there and rot, and if you do put it in the barn after it's been rained on, it can mildew, heat up, and burn the blasted barn down.' He laughed, and old Jasper laughed with him, then he went stamping back out into the soggy yard to lean upon a post-and-rider fence and study the oat field. It hadn't been mowed yet, so at least it was still a usable crop, but it was in the milk, ready for harvesting. Fortunately, too, the rainfall hadn't been accompanied by wind, or otherwise perhaps as much as two-thirds of the crop would have been beaten flat to the ground, destroying it.

While Jasper was out making his professional evaluation, Liz came over to be kissed, then she said, 'We stopped at the bank on the way out. Granddad had seventy-five thousand dollars in there. It's been lying there drawing interest for thirty years, since he sold his farm lands before I was born.' She placed both hands on the hay rake and shook her head slowly. 'I had no idea. It never occurred to me at all. Granddad never mentioned having a fortune, and he certainly never acted the part.'

Jake wiped his hands on a soiled rag. 'But it doesn't seem right, taking his money, sweetheart. I thought about it for a long while last night, when I was lying in bed listening to the rain. It belongs to him and . . . '

Elizabeth held up a small blue passbook with a bank's name and escutcheon upon it. 'Here is our bankbook, Jake. Read it. There is sixty-five thousand dollars in our names in the account. If we need the other ten thousand Granddad said he'd make that over, too.'

Jake didn't take the offered passbook. He continued to wipe on the greasy rag and look solemn. He didn't know what to say, so he said nothing, and in the meantime Liz put up the little book and stood gazing out of a soiled window where the fresh morning sunlight struck like new copper across the drenched, dark fields, and breathed the air that was heavy with a special kind of countryside mustiness.

Jasper ambled back, shot them both a look from beneath shaggy brows, and said, 'You were lucky last night, Jake, it didn't flatten the crop. Probably won't rain again this month, so if you allowed two days for drying, then cut and got her baled, you ought to have a nice hay crop of oats.' Jasper walked closer to them and paused to examine the work being done on the rake. 'She's told you, I suppose, and that accounts for the pair of long faces.' He smiled, leaned on the rake and continued speaking. 'I'm glad to be shed of it, to tell you the truth. I'll hang on to that last ten thousand in case I meet a swishy widow-woman or something.' He stopped, moved his lips doubtfully, then said, 'Excuse me, the word is swinging, not swishy. Hey, what are you two looking so down-at-the-mouth about?'

He did not allow either of them a chance to respond. Old Jasper, who had lived so long, was experienced beyond the understanding of either of the younger people. He knew perfectly well what their problem was. He also knew that allowing them to bring it out would put him on the defensive, which he had no intention of allowing. He had not argued with Jake, but he had with Liz, and he had a wholesome respect for her logic.

'I'm not pushing in,' he said. 'I figured to wait until the wedding, then give you the dowry, but it looked to me as though the farm ought to come first. Anyway, it's kind of hard being lovers when you've got something that momentous on your mind. The point is — it's Liz's inheritance any way you look at it, and if I waited to see she got it until my death-bed day, I can tell you right now the government inheritance tax vultures would be around to take all but the bare bones of it.'

Elizabeth was listening. She was also looking at her grandfather through misty eyes. Jake had finished wiping his hands on the oily cloth, and they did not look any cleaner, but he smiled at old Jasper and shoved out a soiled hand, which the older man grasped, pumped once and released.

'Done,' said old Jasper, in the manner of rural men who had just completed a trade. 'Now I've got to get back. Shall I leave Liz here, or take her back with me?'

Jake's twinkle appeared. 'Mister Carleton, if you expect me to get the mower mounted on the tractor to be ready to start cutting the oats as soon as the ground is dry, you'd better take her back with you. But if you don't think it matters when I start mowing, why not leave her?'

That rather involved answer amused Jasper. He laughed. Elizabeth smiled, and when her grandfather stopped his noise she said, 'I'll stay. I'll go over to the house and start making Jake's mid-day meal, and he's not to come over there until I call him, either.' She turned and walked out of the equipment shed, strode purposefully across the sun-drenched yard with both men watching her through a window, and after she had reached the house Jake said, 'I don't think they ever made but one like her, Mister Carleton.'

Old Jasper had an answer to that. 'They made two more that I can name right off; her grandmother and her mother. And when I was a young man, New England had a lot of them. Kind of hard-headed at times, but you say the right words to 'em and they just sort of melt.'

Jake laughed. Jasper was a long way from being one of those befuddled oldtimers. Whatever he had learned in his long lifetime, he had evidently remembered, if it was anything worth remembering. The last thing he did was wink. Then he went out to his old car, climbed in and went chugging the three miles back to town.

For a while Elizabeth could see Jake working around the equipment shed, then he disappeared and she thought he had gone down to the barn, but she wasn't sure.

She imagined the old Sumner house was her home and decided that the first thing she would do would be brighten up the kitchen. There was room in the rear wall for two more windows, and where the pantry was, off the rear entrance between kitchen and gloomy old rear porch with its assortment of musty overshoes and none-too-clean winter jackets, she thought in terms of a glass door. At least a door that was glass the upper one-half to permit more light inside.

She was thinking of colour combinations for the painting she would do when Jake came in from out back looking pleased about something. He reached for her, but she eluded him.

'You're not supposed to come until I call you for lunch,' she said.

He brought a hand from behind him. On his large palm was a small rabbit with dark spots. It couldn't have been more than a few days old. 'This is Terence,' he told her, as she took the tiny creature and put its warm body against her cheek. 'There are two hutches of them in the barn, but far back where we didn't inventory. Terence has two brothers, Patrick and Michael.'

The rabbit was so small and still. It gained confidence after a while and wrinkled its nose and moved slightly as Elizabeth held it. She said, 'Terence likes me. Look at him nuzzle my hair.' She held the rabbit out to look at it. 'I'll give it some of that rolled oats in the cupboard,' she said, and started to move before Jake stopped her.

'He can't eat yet, only milk. Give him another couple of weeks.' He held out his hand for the small rabbit. 'I'd better take him back or his mother'll be upset. You could come with me and see the others, if you'd like.'

Liz arched a dark brow. 'I've heard about country boys taking girls into barns. It's the rural equivalent of inviting city girls up to see a man's apartment.'

They laughed together, and when

Jake turned to walk back out into the yard, Liz trailed obediently after him, evidently not very fearful of being caught in the barn.

The morning was well advanced and the humidity from wet earth caused steam to arise from the places where hot sunlight struck hardest. It was one of those days when people drank a lot of water — or New England cider, if they preferred it — and avoided manual labour. By the time Liz was two-thirds of the way across the yard with Jake, she could feel the effects of the debilitating humidity. She said something about how a constant environment like this would sap a person's energy, and did not even remotely consider that such an innocent statement would resurrect bleak thoughts, until Jake said, 'Sweetheart, I hope you never have to find out what this kind of humidity is like when it's the same every blessed day, rain, heat, humidity, jungle, leeches fastening to your legs in the swamp-water, and the smell of rotting vegetation with you twenty-four hours a day.'

She saw her mistake at once, but Jake did not adhere to those unpleasant thoughts. As they entered the barn he sighed, signifying that the passage from heat to coolness was some kind of key to his thoughts. He even turned and smiled at her as they trod the spongy layer of mustiness and chaff that had been accumulating in the high-roofed old red barn for many more years than they were old, their ages combined.

When they came to the rabbit hutch, it was in a part of the barn she had never entered before. Nearby was a wall of stacked hay left over from the previous year. It was aromatic. Jake put tiny Terence back with his great, overweight mother, and Terence disappeared almost immediately somewhere among the furry rolls of fat that his mother exuded in all directions. She eyed the two-legged things with an expression of mild tolerance, and when Jake put some rolled barley into a tin inside her cage, she wrinkled her nose at him and did not move.

Jake set the rolled barley tin atop the hutch and made an excuse for the fat female rabbit. 'She's still digesting breakfast. Normally she eats like a pig.'

Liz said, 'An apt simile. Isn't it dangerous for her to be so fat? I heard, as a youngster, that overweight rabbits die of heat prostration in summertime.'

'Not in here,' explained Jake. 'That's why we put the hutches back where the coolest part of the barn was, and where afternoon breezes blow through. Anyway, have you ever heard of a successful rabbit diet?'

They looked in the other cage where another doe, younger and nearly as large but from a different cause, fretfully pulled tufts of hair from her body to line a box inside her cage. Jake said, 'This is — maybe I hadn't better tell you; Rolfe Sumner and I kept her name a secret.'

Liz leaned, studied the grey doe for a moment, then said, 'Aggie?'

'Nope. Eulalia. Rolfe said she's

officious, efficient, has beautiful dark eyes, and gets a little thicker each year.'

Liz laughed, and was scandalised. 'You ought to be ashamed.'

Jake was penitent, with a broad smile. 'Oh, I am. I always laugh when I'm ashamed of myself. Anyway, *he* named her, I didn't.'

Obviously, Eulalia was going to be a mother shortly. Jake did not tarry long at her cage, explaining that does had been known to be so agitated by strangers appearing at their cages before giving birth, they would kill their offspring.

They went back across the old barn in the fragrant coolness, hand-in-hand, Liz content to be alone with Jake like this, and before they reached the doorway she was hanging back just a little.

He stopped and looked quizzically downward. She smiled winsomely. 'You are so wonderfully masculine,' she whispered. 'So strong and tall and tanned — and thick. Kiss me!'

He obeyed, and if he had been a little slow at first, he made up for that with ardour — until a car drove into the yard.

It was a youth who delivered telegrams. The message was from Nebraska. After Jake got rid of the delivery-boy he took the message back to the barn for Liz to read. She looked down, looked up, and said, 'But I thought they were not supposed to come until you sent them the letter. This telegram says they will be flying in tomorrow afternoon.'

Jake's expression was saturnine. 'I warned you, sweetheart, and now you are going to find out for yourself. My father does not take no or maybe for an answer.'

She suddenly forgot all about her earlier thoughts and remembered that she hadn't had her hair done up in two weeks, and that she would need a new dress for this crucial meeting. Still clutching the telegram, which she completely forgot to give back, she said,

'Take me home, Jake, right away. I've got to get ready.'

He was mildly dismayed. 'But it says they won't arrive until tomorrow, Liz.'

'I know. And it's going to take me that long to be presentable. Please . . . ' She grabbed his hand and pulled him out of the barn in the direction of the car. 'Hurry, please.'

He hurried, but he was also baffled. The message clearly stated that his parents would not fly in until the following day.

16

The Day Before

Jasper was like Jake, he did not see anything to get so upset about. Elizabeth left them both in the parlour and flew to her bedroom, and from there out through the back of the house to the garage to drive back uptown to the hairdresser's establishment. It was customary to make an appointment first, but this was an emergency.

Later, with her hair in place, she went to the dress shop next to the bank, made her selection with great care — to the consternation of the elderly soul with the vile disposition who ran the shop — paid for her purchase and drove back home.

Jake and her grandfather were loitering out near the shed, admiring the garden. As she tried on the new dress in her bedroom, and alternately watched her two menfolk from a window, she wondered how long it would take, with both of them working at it, to deplete her grandfather's secret store of home-brew. And next fall, after summer was past and there was frost on the ground, what excuse they would use to go stand out there in the old toolshed.

The dress she had bought comple-mented her taffy hair and blue-eyed beauty very well. It was an autumn shade, which would be more appropri-ate in a couple of months than right now, but she hadn't bought it for that reason; she had bought it because it flattered her figure and her colouring, neither of which actually needed much flattering.

To get an honest reaction, she went out through the back of the house to the rear garden, and approached her lover and her grandfather. They both heard her and turned at the same time. She watched closely. Her grandfather's faded but shrewd old eyes popped wide open. Jake's lips loosened, his eyes brightened with soft yearning, and Elizabeth had her answer without saying a word.

'You're uncommonly like your mother today,' said old Jasper. 'I've never seen you look so much like her before, Lizzie.'

She hated that name with a passion. The children at school had used it to tease her, to make her fighting mad. The only time her grandfather used it was when he forgot, like now, how much she detested it. Now, he was looking at a reflection of someone else named Elizabeth whom he had called Lizzie years ago, and who hadn't minded at all — her mother.

'Pretty as a valentine,' said Jake. 'I'll always remember you like this.' He offered her a hand and she took it, closed her fingers around his thick palm, the nails digging in a little, but he relished that small pain, too. 'I'm not sure waiting a week is such a good idea after all.'

'This is how I'll look tomorrow when we go out to pick up your parents, Jake. Is it all right; I mean, do I look too small-townish?'

'You're prettier than a New York fashion model,' exclaimed Jake, and called for a biased bystander to support him in that contention. 'Mister Carleton, did you ever see a more lovely girl?'

'Nope, and I never saw a more lovely woman, either,' maintained her grandfather. 'I can't answer for the Bartletts, but in my experience they don't come any more handsome.' Old Jasper paused a moment, then said, 'I was just telling Jake that John Foreman called this afternoon, shortly after I got home from the Sumner place. He wants us all to meet at his office tomorrow. Bob Hammond will be there.'

Liz didn't like the sounds of that. 'What for, Granddad? Is it something to do with the farm?'

All old Jasper could say with lucidity was that he had, in fact, got that impression. 'It seems to have quite a little to do with the farm, but John Foreman was a tight-mouthed boy even back when we attended the normal school together, and today, because he's older and a darn sight meaner, he says even less.'

They returned to the house, where Liz excused herself to go and change. While she wrestled out of the new dress and into something less formal she puzzled over what the solicitor would want, and decided it probably had to do with leasing Sumner farm until it could be sold. If that was it, then she was half-inclined to believe Bob Hammond had put old Foreman up to it in order to gain quick control.

She smiled to herself. Bob Hammond was due for a surprise. When she returned to the front of the house Jake said he and her grandfather had decided to take her out to dinner tonight. She hadn't thought about going out, but with her hair freshly set she had no objection. She would have to change back, of course, into the new dress again, but not for a while.

The three of them went out front where recent rainfall had cooled the front of the house, and when Liz offered to make lemonade the men liked that idea. She went back indoors, and she'd hardly gone before Jasper said, 'Well, I've never been to Nebraska, but I've heard they raise lots of corn and cattle there, and that they got some fine big cities and lots of wealth.'

It was all true, but Nebraska was part tame-West and part wild-West. Out where Jake's uncle had his feed-lot the ground was too uneven and flinty for farming, but it grew excellent range feed. Elsewhere, the land was loamy, deep, and unbeatably productive. But, of course, what Jasper was really pondering was what kind of folks they had out there, and specifically what kind would be dropping out of the sky tomorrow.

Jake couldn't exactly reassure him. He told Jasper about the same thing concerning his father that he had told

Elizabeth, and Jasper took it all in without a flicker. He had, he said, known that dynamic-type person before. In fact, if one cared to think back to it, old John Foreman in his youth was that kind, which was probably why he had gone down to the city and had made such a name for himself.

Liz returned with the lemonade. There were a few streaked clouds in the sky which seemed to be hastening westerly as though to a rendezvous where another storm might strike, and there was a faint breath of roiled air, otherwise the land was washed clean and visibility had increased until it was possible, by twisting a little, to look northward and see the mountaintops, complete with their bristle-cone pines up there, and their bluish stands of spruce.

Jasper thought the lemonade was excellent, but the way he looked at the glass in his hand and the way he said that made it appear that he thought more of his homebrew, but Elizabeth frowned and her grandfather said nothing at all about a change.

She wondered aloud whether they ought to put up the Bartletts at the inn, which was in the middle of the village and was very old, or whether they should bring them home to the Carleton place. Jake said, 'What's wrong with taking them out to the farm and putting them up? Lord knows there's plenty of room. Those upstairs bedrooms that haven't been slept in for fifty years.'

Elizabeth looked disapproving. 'Too eerie,' she said. 'Anyway, they won't see much of the village stuck out there.'

Jake shrugged. 'The inn, then. I'll stop by and make reservations on my way to pick you up in the morning.'

Jasper smiled. 'No one's made reservations there since Ethan Allen and his Green Mountain Boys came back from the invasion of Canada during the Rebellion. You'd shock the proprietor.'

They sat comfortably for another

hour or so, then Liz went to change and the men went to wash before going out to dinner. Actually, there were only two eateries in the village, and one of those was for the hamburger trade, which left only one, the Upstate Tavern, for those who wanted to make a special occasion of a dinner out. The Upstate Tavern had been an ale house two hundred years earlier, and pewter mugs hanging from wooden pegs attested to that fact, along with a number of Rebellion-era artifacts, but the proud old tavern had fallen on evil days; the latest proprietor and his wife were very devout members of the Brotherhood of the Holy Ghost sect and allowed nothing stronger than coffee in their establishment. They also had 'No Smoking' signs posted prominently upon every wall.

Their food was good. Earthy, substantial, served hot in ample helpings, as though each diner were part of a harvest crew, but for those like Jasper who liked a mug of dark ale with his dinner, there was instead a choice of tea or coffee.

When Jasper, Jake and Elizabeth arrived it was early for dinner, but that was what they got nonetheless for a very good reason: the Upstate Tavern served only two meals a day, breakfast and dinner. Anyone arriving after breakfast time got dinner regardless of the time of day, eleven in the morning or two in the afternoon.

Jake, who had never eaten at the tavern before, was impressed by the black, aged old oaken rafters and the uneven plastercoat between upright wall-studs. The ceiling was low, the floor was of worn and uneven flagstone, and there was a great old fireplace filling nearly a third of one wall. It was easy, Jake whispered to Liz, to picture Continental officers in blue tunics and white gaiters, standing here toasting 'The Cause' on bitter winter nights with their backs to a roaring fire.

She said it did not have to be all

imagination, that the old tavern had a quite colourful history. Her grandfather knew most of the legends, having heard them as a boy, but she did not encourage him otherwise their dinner would have been prolonged until after dark, and she had something else in mind, at least for two of them, after dinner — a drive up to the bluff on the yonder side of the river.

The meal was roast beef cooked to perfection, fresh vegetables, dark bread with home-made butter as yellow as new gold, and coffee, tea, or milk, and an apple cobbler for dessert. Liz stopped mid-way through, Jasper quit after his beef was gone but before his vegetables gave out, and even Jake had to yield when he got to the dessert. The helpings were too large for normal appetites; for people who were just passing through, or people like the Carletons and Jake Bartlett who hadn't exercised much this day, the amount of food was needlessly excessive. Jasper said the proprietor's wife, who did all the cooking and baking and even made the butter herself, operated on the theory that if the good Lord would tend to the souls of her patrons, she would tend to the appetites.

Liz hadn't said very much throughout the meal. She was thinking ahead to what was, in her view anyway, the critical new day to come. She was going to marry Jake whether his parents liked her, or approved of him getting married, or not, but she wanted very much for them to approve at least of her.

He had told her as much as was necessary for her to form opinions, tentative ones at any rate, of what his parents were like. She was prepared to like his mother and to fear his father. She even tried to imagine what they would look like, and concluded that Jake's father would be an older edition of Jake, and his mother would be a small, stocky, robust woman with dark hair and dark eyes. She had no basis for these images, but she had them, and until they were proven incorrect she would keep them.

Jake surmised what her silence meant, but he was discreet. Not until he and Jasper had split the tab, something old Jasper insisted upon, did he mention the coming event at all, and even then, as he held the chair for her to arise, all he did was lean close as she came up to her feet and whisper in her ear.

'Relax. There is nothing short of Divine Providence that can change anything where you and I are concerned.'

They met some villagers coming in as they were going out, whom Jasper and his grand-daughter knew, had known most of her life in fact. It was finally getting late enough for the regular supper trade to be appearing. As a rule, like most villages and small towns, folks ate out only on Saturday night, making a kind of special weekly event of it. This applied in Washington, Vermont, too, but there were a few, like Everette De

Pugh, who had wives who were terrible cooks; those diners ate out at every opportunity. It was that, or risk ptomaine poisoning.

Liz saw the way people's eyes drifted from her to Jake. She wanted to smile; instead she acted as though she could not guess how the villagers' minds were turning. Well, people had to have something to whisper about, and if they were talking about her, then they weren't talking about someone else, and right at this point she didn't really care very much. She had something infinitely more pressing to worry about.

They drove back home and Jasper sprang out and closed the car door with a wink and a smile. 'Too nice a night to waste inside watching television with me,' he said. 'It was very nice, having supper like that. I'll probably see the pair of you tomorrow. By the way, I got the impression from John Foreman he only wanted you two at the meeting at his office, so suppose I sort of sashay your folks around the countryside while you two are at the conference?'

Jake thought that was a good idea, if it didn't put Jasper out any. He scoffed. 'That's probably the one thing I do best — guide folks around.' He looked at Elizabeth, his smile gentle. Then he winked, turned without another word and went hastening towards the dark house.

As Jake drew away from the kerbing he said, 'I wish they could all be like your grandfather. He's one in a million.'

Liz agreed, but only with a nod because she had a lump in her throat.

17

The Night Before

They passed two cars, each one of them parked at a lay-by part way up towards the overhead top-out of the cliff, and although Liz had misgivings, when they reached the place where they usually left the car, they were the only people up there, which was unusual in a way, and yet because it was the middle of the week, and also because there just were not all that many romantic young people in the village, in another way it was not unusual.

The night was less warm than other times they had been to this place, but it was not cold nor even chilly as Liz and Jake strolled ahead, hand-in-hand, to look down where the river flowed, and on across, slightly northward, where village lights and shadows were.

As though she had spoken her thoughts, he said, 'Don't worry so much, sweetheart. Tomorrow will come and go and you and I won't be changed.'

Maybe they wouldn't be changed, she thought, but a man and his parents should be close; she did not want to be the cause for any kind of family rift. 'Something will be changed,' she responded. 'Just meeting them is bound to make some kind of a change, Jake. And I'm worried about Mister Foreman wanting to have this conference — us and Bob Hammond — too.'

He smiled. 'Bad premonition?'

That was just it, she had no premonition at all. 'Suppose Hammond has worked some shenanigan and got control of the farm?'

Jake was unconcerned. 'How? It would have to be advertised in the newspaper, and I'd have to be served eviction notice. Stop worrying so much; you're going to end up with an ulcer.'

She smiled over at him. Hardly that, she wasn't that type, and worrying, with her, was neither a habit nor even a temporary condition — up until now, at any rate, it hadn't been.

He leaned on a stone rampart where the guard-chain attached, then dropped for a hundred feet before being attached to another rampart. The stars were closer than usual because of the fresh-washed air. The moon was unimpressive, but there were enough stars to make up the diminished brilliance, and where light leapt back upwards from the flowing river it was like a tarnished reflector.

She leaned until they touched and said, 'A penny for your thoughts.'

He grinned without turning. 'They're worth a lot more.'

'A kiss, then?'

He finally turned. 'Sold. Do I collect first, or afterwards?'

She slid an arm under his jacket and round his lean waist. 'Afterwards.'

'I was thinking whether to name our

first son Jacob Bartlett or Jasper Bartlett.'

She slid the other arm round him and leaned closer without speaking. A car came up over the top of the bluff but sped onward into the northward night, its fading sound growing fainter until the silence returned. Still Liz did not speak.

'Maybe we should name him Jasper,' said Jake, 'and the second boy Jacob. But what shall we name the girls?'

Elizabeth pulled up and raised her face to him. 'How many are you thinking about?'

He shrugged in her embrace. 'Four to six. What is your opinion?'

'One at a time,' she said, and ducked her face to hide the rising colour. 'Otherwise I don't care, boys or girls.' She snuggled inward and clung fiercely to him. 'I hope they can grow up in Vermont, tramping the woods and camping at the lakes . . . and never have to go to war, Jake.'

He nodded. 'Amen.'

Another car came up over the topout and went swiftly across the level area, then shot down the far side, heading northward. He said whatever it was that drew people this far from the cities must be particularly alluring tonight. It was the distant lakes and mountains, she thought, because this was the usual holiday time for city-folk. Usually, they did not leave the broad, new carriageways, but now and then some venturesome soul swung off and went through the village, then crossed the river at the steel bridge and took the bluff road northward to an intersecting juncture with the carriageway again, many miles northward, up near the State Capitol.

'What happened to the brave new world that was supposed to come out of the last large war?' she asked. 'What happened to the new ecology, the new life for us all that the students and nature-nuts were going to bring forth?'

With a soft hint of cynicism he said, 'The same thing that always happens:

failure, because there are no real, wide divergencies possible. The world changes an inch, or a moment, at a time, and all the new-era advocates since the Year One haven't been able to speed up the process one second.'

He lifted her face. She saw moonlight reflected in his eyes, saw the softness come to his lips as he sought her mouth, and just before she closed her eyes she saw his wide shoulders block out a large part of the sky.

It never failed. When he kissed her she had that peculiar sensation of being at the vortex of a silent, great explosion. Afterwards, she was a little weak and a little breathless, and clung to him.

'We'll do the best we can,' he told her quietly. 'We'll raise them to be self-reliant, tough and resourceful. I don't know how else we can prepare them for life, do you?'

She shook her head while her face was against his chest. She remembered finding a book on raising children her grandfather had got at the library, years ago, and she also remembered reading a little from it, but particularly the preface, which said that if parents taught their children to be honest, and if they never managed to teach them anything else, it would be the greatest accomplishment parents could ever accomplish.

But she said nothing of this, because it appeared that Jake's ideas were more far-reaching, more ambitious. She would wait and see.

'I guess the real new world,' he mused, 'is here and now. It's the world you and I will make together.'

She could have agreed heartily with that, because it had also occurred to her that love *is* a new world; she had thought of that several days back, but it seemed an age ago, now that she was committed to him, an age ago when she'd been a girl instead of a woman.

He held her at arms' length. 'For better or for worse,' he said, and smiled, then dropped his arms from her shoulders. 'Any regrets, so far?'

She had none, and could imagine having none. 'Just that tomorrow night — well — might make a difference, somehow, and that's a fear, not a regret.'

He took one of her hands and turned, taking her gently along as he paced slowly northward along the top of their high place. 'I told you, stop worrying about tomorrow,' he reiterated. 'It will be just another day, with two fresh personalities in it, but as far as we are concerned it can't be terribly different.'

He was wrong. How wrong neither of them would know until long after his parents had arrived, but right then, full of resolve and love atop the bluff, he had every right to speak, and to feel, as he did.

They walked onward until the slope loomed ahead, and below it a tangled kind of night-shadow made by trees and riverside undergrowth, then they paused, considering a narrow footpath chewed deep into the stone.

She explained that pathway. 'The legend has it that in prehistoric times, and even up until about the founding of our village — which was called New Lincoln before the Rebellion — Indians used this path to come up here to speak to Manitou, their Great Spirit, and to also light signal fires. The last ones to come up here — and this is pure fiction, according to my grandfather and some of the oldtimers who heard a different story from their grandfathers — were surrounded by frontiersmen and forced to die by gunfire up here or jump into the river. Most jumped, and all were killed.'

Jake nodded. 'In Nebraska we have one or two stories of genuine massacres, and fifty legends of more gory ones that never happened at all.'

Liz went over and put a foot into the deep-scored footpath. 'Whether the surround took place or not, look how deep this is; wouldn't you say the path was very old?'

He laughed and said, 'Sweetheart, it's

an old path, but you should remember that rainwater and snow-runoff would also follow down the runnel of that trail, cutting deeper and deeper into the sandstone.'

She straightened up. 'Spoilsport! I was ready to visualise a single-file line of painted, feathered Algonquins or Senecas stalking up the slope from down where they'd left their canoes.'

'You'd better visualise some support for us, then,' he laughed. 'Or at least a pair of automatic rifles.' He held his hand out, she took it and they turned back. 'What happened to your Indians?' he asked. 'In my hometown the guy who owns the lumberyard is a Sioux, and the local dentist is a Blackfeet.'

She had heard rumours of who had Indian blood, and who had an Indian ancestor or two but never mentioned it, but all she could say was: 'I don't, as far as I know, but I wouldn't care to make any great wagers about that. Ask my grandfather; it's the older people who know which closets to shake to rouse up a rattling skeleton or two.'

As they got back to the car another vehicle came to the topout, and this one slowed, then swung out on to the flat place a number of yards from their car. Liz was sure she would recognise the passengers in that car if they got out, but they didn't. In fact, they doused their lights and sat in the dingy gloom without even making a sound. Jake leaned and muttered, 'Lovers; for shame,' and winked at her as they covered the last few yards to his car. 'It's unhealthy to sit in a car with all the windows rolled up,' he added.

She cocked her head at him. 'But fun.'

He stifled a laugh, held the door for her, and, after she was in, he leaned to kiss her, then drew back, closed the door and went round to his side to slide in at her side. He sat a moment without moving, then raised his head. She knew his thoughts and pointed a rigid finger towards the ignition switch. 'We are going home now,' she said, enunciating so clearly that it amused him.

They backed around, swung southward and eased gently down off the topout. As they slowed to creep across the steel bridge she leaned low and shot a look upwards where they had come from. It was dark up there, no lights showed at all.

Jake caught her doing that. 'Hey, who appointed you to police the morals of the village?'

Her answer was pointed. 'No one. And that's not what I was doing. I'm just curious to see who *she* was.'

They laughed together. He accused her of being just like some of the older women around Washington. She did not deny it. 'What do you expect from a small-town girl but a small-town woman? And you'd be curious, too, if you knew everyone in town.'

He did not deny it. 'I'm curious, and I don't even know her — or him. But I've always thought life in country villages was sedate, very moral and dignified, and a crushing drag.'

She had a practical answer for him. 'Well, lover, you've had your share of life in a country village lately. Do you *still* think it's such a drag?'

He blushed, and she was so surprised, having never seen him do that before, that she giggled. He kept looking straight ahead, acting as though neither thing had happened, acting as though he was thinking only of driving up out front of her home.

If they hadn't been down in the lighted part of town she wouldn't have seen that blush. Even so, it was little more than a glimpse. She slid over next to him, kissed his cheek and put her head upon his shoulder. 'I'm sorry, I didn't mean to embarrass you. Anyway, now you know that life in a hick town is no different from life anywhere else, except that perhaps there just aren't as many of the hicks.'

They pulled up out front of the dark house, and he said her grandfather must retire early. It was midnight by her watch, and very few houses in the neighbourhood showed lights, meaning that just about everyone else was also abed. But she made no issue of his comment as they left the car and he walked her up to the porch. She was readying for what was to come. When they reached the door he swung her gently, pressed his lips to her mouth before she had ceased moving, and with a burst of fiery ardour let her know exactly how he felt.

She did not flinch; she had met his passions before and was their match, but she held him longer than usual, and when she finally let him draw away for breath, she said, 'I'm shaking in my boots about tomorrow and don't tell me that I shouldn't, because I can't help it.' Then she pushed him with both hands. 'Go get some rest, sweetheart, and be back here for me after breakfast. Okay?'

He said, 'Okay. Just remember one thing: I love you.'

18

A Letdown

The last three words Jake spoke to her buoyed her up until he arrived the following morning, but as they were driving towards that emergency airstrip on the outskirts of town she began to have that sinking sensation again.

Later, when they had been parked beside the runway for a half-hour, and had walked among the empty, unpainted wooden hangars and tie-down sites, his presence raised her spirits, until, shortly before eleven o'clock, they heard the incoming aircraft, and she saw it, when Jake aimed his arm against the sun, sleeky and shiny, red-and-white, tilting down across a pale morning sky towards the landing area, then her courage leaked away again.

Jake's father was obviously an experienced flyer. He swung left, then right, until he was hovering over the strip, and very effectively let down without a bump, touched ground and ran out his landing distance. He came to a stop no more than two hundred feet from where Jake and Elizabeth waited, hand-in-hand.

As soon as the plane's passengers alighted Liz saw that she had been right in one way, and wrong in another. Jake's father was indeed an older Jake Bartlett, tanned and lean and fit-looking, a little more hawk-eyed, definitely more commanding and assertive. But his mother was not a small dark woman, she was rather tall, about Liz's size, and she had blue eyes, not brown ones. She also had a very warm smile when the four of them came together and Jake made the introductions. Liz could feel the curiosity behind the smiles, but at least Mrs Bartlett held her hand a moment longer than was necessary, and gave her fingers a little squeeze of understanding and, perhaps, sympathy.

Jake and his father tied down the aircraft. His mother, standing with Liz, said they had arisen before dawn at a town several hundred miles distant in order to make the flight on time, and she was starved. She laughed about that.

'You'll learn someday that when a man makes up his mind to go somewhere, if you delay him too long or too many times, he'll stop asking you. I'm used to missing a meal. It's been worth it.'

Their eyes met, and Elizabeth saw the friendly but honest interest in her the older woman felt. She had expected nothing less, actually, and as the four of them were going towards Rolfe Sumner's dusty car, Mrs Bartlett looked at the distant mountains, at the heat-hazed distant village, and said it was a picturesque countryside, and she remembered some of how it was from pictures her mother had showed her.

Her parents had gone to Nebraska from Vermont something like forty years ago.

Jake explained about Sumner farm on the slow drive to town. His father listened, his blunt profile visible to Elizabeth, who sat in the back with Mrs Bartlett, and when Jake had finished Elizabeth got her first inkling of Mr Bartlett's personality, exactly as Jake had described it.

The elder Bartlett said, 'Who is Hammond? How does he think he's going to steamroller his way in when you've already got the inside track?'

Liz answered for Jake. 'Mister Hammond is a wealthy and successful local farmer, Mister Bartlett. He's no one to take lightly. He has a reputation of getting what he goes after.'

Mister Bartlett turned and smiled at Elizabeth. 'Nothing wrong with initiative nor ambition, Elizabeth, unless of course they interfere with what *we* want, is there?'

Liz heard her answer and was surprised. 'Mister Bartlett, it's not what we want, it's what Jake wants.'

Jake's father's eyes narrowed slightly in appraisal. 'Okay,' he said, 'it's what Jake wants. But we're his family, and families stick together. As far as Hammond is concerned, maybe amongst us we can finance Mister Hammond right out of the picture. Doesn't that make sense to you?'

Liz smiled straight into the elder Bartlett's narrowed eyes. 'It makes sense to me, yes, sir, but only if it comes from Jake, in the form of a request.'

They continued to look at one another for a long moment, then Jake eased the car to the kerbing outside the shaded old Carleton house and everyone alighted. Old Jasper came out on to the porch up across the yard looking very tidy in a fresh white shirt and tan trousers. For someone who seemed unflappable, old Jasper wiped both hands on the seams of his trousers, looking self-conscious as the handsome woman and greying man strode on up to be introduced.

They stood a moment on the porch where a slight morning breeze played, then went indoors, and Liz would have gone to make lunch but her grandfather scotched that, and he was sufficiently emphatic about it to prevent her from arguing. He was going to take the Bartletts down to the village to luncheon, and if Jake and Liz didn't hurry they'd be late for the conference at John Foreman's office, which was a glassed-in half-section of the front porch of the splendid, three-storey old Foreman residence over on Elm Street, one block behind the commercial area.

As Jake and Liz turned to leave, Jake's father said, 'If you need backing, son, remember that you've got it.' He looked at Liz and smiled. 'But I don't anticipate anyone getting the better of the *pair* of you.' It was, Liz thought, a kind of oblique, tough-minded signal of the elder Bartlett's approval of her, but not as a girl and a prospective daughter-in-law, as much as his approval of a tough-minded woman.

On the way to the car she wanted to tell Jake that she had made a bad first impression, but she didn't get a chance because he told her he had seen the look of approval on his mother's face. That was something she could feel grateful for. The other thing was that as her grandfather took the elder Bartletts on a tour of the village and the countryside this afternoon, he would do his best to sell her to them.

Still, as they drove away, she felt depressed and Jake inevitably noticed it. He was mildly distressed. 'Shake it off, sweetheart, you're doing just fine so far.'

She smiled at him. 'I'm glad you think so. I'm afraid I was waiting for an excuse to cross swords with him. We had hardly got out of the airport yard than I went after him.'

Jake laughed. 'You're imagining things. You expressed an opinion was all. He likes that in people. He never expects everyone to agree with him. You should hear some of the arguments he and my brother Jim get into.'

She wasn't up to any kind of an argument, and as they turned down to Elm Street and she saw the soiled but late model car parked out front of the Foreman place, she had to reach way down for her spirit and haul it up manually just to be prepared for some more unpleasantness.

John Foreman, not a very tall man even in his prime before he had settled with age, admitted them to the front of the house and took them to his glassed-in office where a fire was going in the oil-burner even though it was amply warm without it. Bob Hammond arose when the newcomers arrived. He nodded briskly at Liz, then turned a bold, hard look upon Jake, and barely moved his head at all. Jake smiled indulgently and John Foreman, looking annoyed, went behind an oak desk, sifted through some papers and put on a pair of half-submerged glasses he found, then leaned upon the desk and said, 'The purpose of this meeting is to acquaint both of you young men with the requirements of the law respecting the old Sumner place. In the face of what appears a lack of a will and final testament by Rolfe Sumner, the Commonwealth of Vermont can only lease the land on a month-to-month basis to someone, presumably one of you gentlemen, based upon a realistic bid. But this is also to inform you that as court-appointed executor of the Sumner estate I am still going through Rolfe Sumner's papers looking for some clue as to what Rolfe figured was a decent disposal of his effects. If I find nothing, then the land-lease can probably, at the discretion of the Commonwealth Attorney General, be set at an annual rate, with perhaps an option to buy included.' John Foreman paused and cleared his throat. He also peered at Jake and over at Bob Hammond, the old eyes behind his glasses dagger-sharp and yeasty.

'But in the event there is no last testament, and I am beginning to believe this may be the case, I am authorised to solicit bids from you two gentlemen, as the people most pertinently involved, for the farm.'

Foreman removed his rimless glasses and polished them upon an immaculate handkerchief while he eyed Hammond and Jake Bartlett. Then he swung his attention to Elizabeth. 'I understand that you are prepared to bid along with Mister Bartlett, Liz. Your grandfather told me that this morning.'

Hammond finally broke his long, grim silence. 'What's she got to do with it? You said Bartlett and I were pertinent involvees, or something like that, John. If you let her in, you may as well advertise it in the paper and let everyone bid.'

Foreman placed the glasses back upon his nose with great care, peered through them at Bartlett and said, 'Because as I understand it, Bob, it will be partly her dowry that will buy the farm.'

Hammond looked around quickly,

evidently surprised. 'Elizabeth Carleton — going to marry *him*?'

Jake laughed at Hammond's surprise and disgust, otherwise Hammond's remark might not have set so well. Before Liz could speak the lawyer said, 'Bob, she can marry the man in the moon for all I care. This is a law office, not a matrimonial agency. What I want from you is a bid on the Sumner place — that is, if you are interested. Well . . . ?'

Hammond fidgeted. 'Here? Out in the open, right now? I thought those things were done by sealed bid.'

Foreman's testiness rose a notch. 'For heaven's sake, Bob, this isn't a competitive thing, and it's not binding anyway until the Attorney General okays it, and until you boys put up some cash. Well . . . ?'

'Forty thousand,' growled Hammond, and looked menacingly from beneath bushy brows.

Foreman turned. 'Mister Bartlett?'

'Fifty thousand.'

Hammond snarled. 'This here is cash money we're talking about, hired hand.'

Elizabeth said, 'We understand that, Mister Hammond.'

At once the successful farmer, some years older than Jake but also some years younger than John Foreman, raised a cocked eyebrow. 'Oh, I forgot. He's using your money, isn't he? Well, that makes a pretty good trade, he gets the money and you thrown in, like buying the cow and getting the calf for nothing.'

John Foreman sprang to his feet, his face darkening, but he wasn't fast enough. Jake had Bob Hammond, a burly, heavy-set man, lifted two-thirds out of his chair with one hand. 'I think that's enough,' Jake said. 'The mistake people make with bullies, Mister Hammond, is letting them go the first time. Now this was the second time. The third time — and I'll tear your head off.' He dropped Hammond back into his chair and settled back just as John Foreman laced into them both.

For Liz, the suddenness of Jake's movement and the softness of his voice in anger gave her an ample demonstration of that temper of his she had wondered about. She approved of it.

Hammond was red in the face, but John Foreman gave him no chance to retaliate. 'Bob, I told you before these folks arrived that I'd stand for no nonsense this afternoon, and by gawd I meant every word of it. Now you mind your tongue in here or we'll just forget this meeting and the bidding. Is that clear?'

Foreman probably did not expect an answer, but in any case he did not get one. Hammond gathered his coat closer and settled deeper into his chair without taking his eyes off a calendar picture of a mill-wheel over John Foreman's head.

The interlude was past. Jake winked at Liz and she winked back. John Foreman wrote a moment on a yellow, lined tablet, then said, 'Bob, because you adjoin the Sumner land, you are entitled to have the last bid.' At Liz's and Jake's shocked expression, old Foreman raised and dropped his thin little pointed shoulders. 'That is the law. I can only interpret it, not change it. Well, Bob . . . ?'

'What was Bartlett's bid again, John?'

'Fifty thousand dollars cash.'

Hammond turned very slowly and looked steadily at Jake as he said, 'Fifty-five thousand dollars, cash.'

Foreman wrote a moment, then put down the pen and looked up. 'Mister Bartlett, there is only one way you can bid again. That is to go to court and call for a public sale of the Sumner farm. Would you do that?'

Jake arose slowly. Behind him, Liz also stood up. Jake's face was pale, his eyes were dark and hard. 'Mister Foreman, I'm unfamiliar with Vermont law, but I don't think I'm going to sit here and tell you and Mister Hammond what I plan to do.'

Foreman sighed. 'As you wish. I only carry out my duties as defined by the courts.' He stood up and nodded flintily at both Jake and Liz, who left the office and walked down the porch steps without a backward glance. Back in the office, Bob Hammond rose and went to stand by the window to watch the others get into Rolfe Sumner's car and drive off. Then Hammond said, 'Will he make a fight of it?'

Old Foreman, writing at his desk, answered without even looking up. 'After the way you acted, Bob, I hope so. And I'll tell you something else, too. I wouldn't represent either one of you!'

19

Hopes and Fears

Jake and Liz did not drive directly back to the Carleton residence. Jasper would have the Bartletts on a tour of the community anyway, so no one would be there, but that exerted no influence; Jake and Liz did not seek sympathy nor advice in their disturbed frame of mind.

He headed southward out of town and across the steel bridge, then up atop the riverside bluff. There, where they had spent some of their best moments together, he told her he had a bad feeling that Bob Hammond was going to run up the bid on the Sumner place another ten or fifteen thousand dollars, which would put them in a poor bargaining position.

She agreed, but she was far from demoralised. 'We can go that high. Of course, we'll have to get the rest of the money from granddad, or perhaps as a loan from your parents.'

He nodded, having already arrived at these conclusions. 'Also, we need a Vermont lawyer, someone who can guide us through this public-bid business. I think I'd better drive over to Edgerton in the morning and organise our strategy. Hammond isn't going to yield.'

She agreed. 'He'll have several advantages and I don't like that.' She looked over at Jake. 'Maybe we ought to prepare ourselves for losing, Jake. Maybe we ought to start looking at other farms that can be bought.'

He turned and smiled. 'You're probably right, but let's put that off until I've made the run up to Edgerton and talked to an attorney. Our first choice is Sumner farm. No matter how good the next place is, we're still going to look at it as an alternative, and that's no way to buy a farm.' He opened the door, got out of the car and waited a moment until she had also alighted, then they went ahead to the guard-chain and stood over there in afternoon sunshine, each silent with brooding thoughts.

After a while Jake said, 'If he'd just left the farm to an heir somewhere, we could perhaps buy it that way. This intestate thing sounds terribly drawn-out and complicated.'

She remembered John Foreman's attitude and decided the Sumner estate was indeed going to be a complicated affair. She wished heartily for a short moment that Jake had gone to work for someone else, but wishful thinking was no good, so she concentrated on what was their particular problem, trying to imagine some solution. 'At least,' she said, 'you have as good a chance to lease it as Hammond has. Better, I should think, since you're already living out there and working the land.'

He leaned on the guard-chain and gazed steadily northward. It seemed that he was looking towards the village, but Liz knew better than that; he was gazing three miles farther northward. As she studied his tough-set profile she decided there was no alternative; he had to possess the Sumner place and not some secondary choice. She sighed to herself because she had a feeling they were in for a hard fight.

Thinking this way, she said, 'Well, Jake, I suppose it's our foretaste of the future, isn't it? I mean, before we're even married, we have to face a crisis together.' She smiled, and that made him look round and loosen a little, in the hot sunlight.

He smiled back. 'You had no idea life was going to be like this the first time you saw me.'

'If that's some kind of apology, forget it,' she retorted. 'The old life was becoming pretty darned dull. I was beginning to wonder if I had any future at all, beyond keeping house for Granddad.' She leaned to be kissed. 'I'm looking forward to this fight. Bob Hammond's got the *pair* of us to put up with, and you heard what your father said when we left the house.'

He kissed her just as a car sounded down the far north side of the bluff. They pulled apart swiftly, the car breasted the top-out, a female face looked over at them briefly, then the car hastened on across and down the far side. Elizabeth laughed. 'If she had seen us kissing, by this evening it would be all over town, with embellishments. That was Jane De Pugh, wife of the telephone company's local office manager and one of the most active gossips in town.'

Jake was not particularly impressed. He had seen the woman in town before now, but had not known who she was until now. There were a fairly large number of people he knew like that, by sight but not by name. They had not troubled him. There was something else more pressing to worry about. He took Liz by the hand and strolled southward along the rim of their high place, as though it belonged to them, and indeed they were occasionally entitled to think of the cliff-top in that light since only once, in all the trips they'd made up to that place, had intruders appeared.

Where he stopped they could see the steel bridge and the wide, straight flow of the river southward. Down there, defined by fence-rows that were marked by large old trees, were more farms, more distant old houses in rustic settings where people for generations had tilled the soil and raised families. She showed him her grandfather's farm, the one he had sold many years ago. 'Three hundred acres, with one hundred up the far side-hill where the maple trees were. He was born there, but as soon as he got married he bought the house in the village.'

Jake turned. 'Maybe that's what we ought to do, live in the village and farm the land by commuting.'

She made a face at him. 'I was looking forward to having chickens and rabbits and things of my own, out there. And — have you paid any attention to that large rear yard with the picket fence around it?'

He looked steadily at her, baffled for a moment. 'Sure. It's got tangled grass and weeds growing all over . . . Are you thinking about that fenced-in yard the same way I'm thinking about it?'

She blushed and smiled, then turned and pulled him back the way they had come, by the hand. 'Anyway, commuting three miles — six miles round-trip — every day, would be a burden, especially in autumn when the darkness arrives about four o'clock in the afternoon.' She looked round and saw his brooding expression, and wondered if he had heard anything she'd said; he obviously was thinking of their chances of owning Sumner farm. If his expression was any indication of his hopes and convictions, he wasn't too sure they were going to win out.

Perhaps it was foolish to plan the way she was doing, but that was what life for the young was all about, planning, trying to look ahead, guessing, and dreaming. If that was taken away, nothing much was left. She refused to accept the possibility of defeat.

'No matter how much we have to borrow,' she told him, 'we'll still be fifty or sixty thousand dollars ahead, won't we?'

He was slow explaining what was bothering him about beating Hammond and gaining possession of the farm. 'It's the debt, Liz. I realise all newlyweds start out in debt, but not as much as we're probably going to have to borrow. Maybe, if we let the farm go and concentrated on a house in the village, and maybe later on . . .'

She was shaking her head long before he'd finished. 'You'd never be happy retrenching, Jake. We'd be giving up our best dreams . . . What about the large back yard?'

He slid an arm round her waist as they approached the car. 'You're right. For a minute there I let doubt take the reins.' He opened the door on her side, waited until she got in, then closed the door and leaned down. 'You're the best medicine a man could have, did you know that?' He pecked at her cheek, then drew back and went round to slide under the wheel beside her. 'I suppose my folks will be settled at the inn by now. They'll be anxious to hear how we came out with Hammond and John Foreman.'

They drove down off the bluff, southward, and made the rather abrupt turn at the bottom to cross the steel bridge. A flock of wild mallards, evidently feeding in the shade beneath the bridge, started up with a great beating of wings. The car clattering above them on the old bridge must have been responsible. Jake and Liz paused to watch the shiny, plump ducks go beating their way downriver barely high enough off the water to avoid striking it.

Jake smiled and Liz saw the pleased look, was made aware of Jake's honest simplicity; he liked what was basic and honest. So did she.

They drove on as far as the Carleton place, and to their surprise they found his mother and father there on the porch with Jasper. Both his parents had changed into loafing clothes, so they had been installed at the inn with their luggage, obviously, and as Liz remembered his mother's hunger, and saw no sign of it now, it was also apparent that everyone had been fed.

As Jake and Elizabeth walked on up, three older sets of eyes studied them. For Liz it was like being the prize heifer at the county fair, but she braved it out well enough.

Jake's father dived right to the point. 'Well, how did the conference go?'

They gave him all the details as Jake drew up two more chairs. Mister Bartlett did not seem the slightest bit disheartened, which surprised Liz. Then, when he spoke, she understood.

'The first round goes to Mister Hammond,' he said, almost casually. 'That's not so unusual. But now comes the second round, and it seems to me that what you kids need is a sharp lawyer.'

Mister Bartlett's eyes actually sparkled; he was enjoying this impending scrap. Liz made up her mind then and there that Bob Hammond was not in Mister Bartlett's class at all.

Jake's mother broke in with surprising force and resolution. She was such a cheerful woman, had such a nice, open smile it was hard to imagine her over-riding her husband, but that is exactly what she did when she said, 'That'll be enough of that kind of talk for now. Elizabeth, your grandfather showed us some of your school art-work, and told us what a wonderful cook you are.'

Liz shot old Jasper an astonished look. That art-work had been tucked away and forgotten for years, and anyway it wasn't that good. Liz was embarrassed. Old Jasper was very busy studying the rooftop of the house across the road through the trees and did not seem to even have heard.

Mrs Bartlett went on speaking. 'When I was your age I couldn't fry a decent pancake or make an edible omelette. Jake is lucky.' She paused, then said, 'We saw the Sumner farm; it's in a wonderful setting. Even my husband fell in love with it, and that's saying a lot because he ordinarily dislikes mountains closing him in.'

Elizabeth said there was a lot of work to be done on the old house. Mrs Bartlett knew about that, too. When she'd married Jake's father they had started out in a leaky old Nebraska ranch-house that took wind through every crack in the walls and couldn't be heated unless every stove was fired up simultaneously, then someone had to get up every couple of hours all night long in wintertime to keep stocking them, or the waterpipes would freeze and burst.

Mr Bartlett laughed in recollection. 'And the coyotes would come right up into the yard in the snow and she'd swear they were wolves and keep a rifle in the kitchen.'

Mrs Bartlett defended herself and everyone smiled. 'I wasn't raised in the country. My family lived in the city, down in Omaha. We'd never seen anything like coyotes in the yard at the edge of the house.' She looked brightly at Elizabeth. 'I'll tell you a secret — I cried myself to sleep wondering whatever had gotten into me, to make me fall in love with a madman who had to live in draughty old houses way out in the country.'

Jasper slapped his leg and said something Liz had never heard before. 'Elizabeth's grandmother said the self-same thing one time when we were snowed in for two weeks out on the farm. The following spring I bought this house in town.'

Jake was amused. So was Liz. It was interesting, and it was also revealing, to hear these older people talk of *their* tribulations. It made the difficulty about the Sumner farm seem less serious.

The sun was setting, daylight would

linger for some time yet, but it was close to supper time. Jake's father held up a hand when Liz mentioned starting dinner. 'This time,' he said, 'let Mrs Bartlett and me do the honours. They serve a real meal at that tavern.'

Jake nodded, so Liz did not insist on getting dinner. She would have plenty of time, probably, to prove that Mrs Bartlett's remark about her being a good cook was true.

They went indoors, where the Bartletts had left their jackets, and there Elizabeth saw the tell-tale pair of empty homebrew bottles. Her grandfather had served his guests in the house, evidently, instead of taking them out back to the old toolshed, the way he did with Jake.

Liz wondered for the dozenth time when the supply of home-made beer would run dry. What she did not realise was that in his spare time, lately, her grandfather had started another batch working. It would be ready to be bottled just about the time the current supply was gone.

20

For Liz, A Day of Dismay

Liz had charge of the Bartletts the next day. Her grandfather sent her to the inn with his old car, and Jake had told her over the telephone to show his parents the view from the bluff, and whatever sights her grandfather hadn't got around to showing them, while Jake was over in Edgerton hiring an attorney. Liz was both uneasy and self-conscious when she picked up the Bartletts right after breakfast, and headed southward towards the steel bridge with them.

It was Jake's mother who put Liz at ease. She said her husband had eaten eleven hotcakes for breakfast, and had probably gained at least two pounds. All three of them laughed. Mrs Bartlett had a knack for saying things that hardly seemed to warrant being said at all, and which made others laugh. She had a delightful sense of humour. She was also very relaxed and easy to be with. Mr Bartlett, after they reached the cliff-top and stood up there looking around, seemed not to be quite as domineering as Liz had guessed him to be the day before. Maybe his wife had given him a talking to, or maybe Liz had created a kind of benevolent ogre where only a strong-willed man existed.

She showed them the village from the cliff-top, and also the southward run of the little valley. She even pointed out the farm her grandfather had once owned, then took them up where the legendary Indian trail was. She noticed that Jake's father listened to her and watched her with a close, rather intent, interest. Finally, when they were going back to the car, he said, 'I think you're exactly what Jake needs.' He did not elaborate on that, but after they were in the car heading back down the southern slope again, Mr Bartlett seemed more confirmed in his affable attitude towards Elizabeth. She thought he did, anyway, and she certainly wanted him to be.

She took them southward to the end of the little valley, let them see the cattle, all of the dairy variety, kept by farmers down there, then she went back up through the countryside, northward, as far as the village, and swung westerly in mid-town and took them out where an ancient earth-and-stone fortress had once stood, used during the Rebellion as a secret storage facility for lead and gun-powder. Out in that direction, too, they saw what remained of the last sawmill in the area. It was rotting away on its piers and footings, and as though in crowning irony some young pine saplings were growing up through the floor where a huge, rusty old circular saw-blade was frozen to a rusted shaft.

Beyond these sights, the village itself and the river, there was not very much to show people who visited Washington, unless it was the local historical society building, full of musty mementoes and unlikely to be very fascinating to the Bartletts, so Liz made the run back up to the Sumner farm to show Mrs Bartlett the inside of the house, which Jasper hadn't shown them the previous day, and while the women were indoors Mr Bartlett ambled out to peek in the barn, in some of the lesser outbuildings, and fetched up finally where most men lingered longest, in the equipment shed. He was in there when John Foreman drove up out front and went up to knock on the front door. Mr Bartlett went to stand in the shed doorway watching as Elizabeth opened the front door over at the house.

Old Foreman had sunglasses on and had just finished mopping his domed forehead when Liz came to the door and smiled out at him. He didn't smile back, and as usual he got right to business.

'Been some fresh developments,' he said crisply, unaware of the husky man with the bold eyes who was walking over from the equipment shed. 'If you and Jake can make it over to my office later today, maybe around four or five o'clock, we may be able to settle a few things.' John Foreman turned, saw Mr Bartlett, and stared hard at him for a moment, then thrust out a bird-like claw. 'I'm John Foreman, and from the looks of you I'd say you'll be Jake Bartlett's daddy.' They shook and old Foreman finally smiled. 'Look enough alike, don't they, Liz? Well, I'd heard you and Mrs Bartlett had arrived. I hope you enjoy your stay. Glad to have met you. Goodbye, sir.'

Old Foreman withdrew his bony hand, jerked his head up and down, and fled back out through the heat to his car, climbed in and, with a slight wave, drove back out towards the paved road.

Mr Bartlett scratched his neck as he watched the dust. 'He must be the busiest person in town, to rush off like that.'

Liz laughed. 'He's always like that, and he's probably the *least* busy man in town.' She held the door for Jake's father to enter the house, closed it after him and asked if she couldn't fix him a bite of lunch. He wasn't hungry, and made a joke about all those pancakes he'd eaten for breakfast. But there was something else on his mind.

'Foreman wanted you and Jake to have another conference with him. What would it be about, this time, if he's already explained the law's attitude?'

Liz had no idea. 'Unless something new has come up since yesterday. Maybe he's been authorised to lease the farm.'

It was the look on Jake's father's face that made Liz wonder, otherwise she wouldn't have thought too much about John Foreman's request.

'It's nothing trivial,' said Mr Bartlett. 'That nervous a man wouldn't go to all the trouble of hunting you up and driving out here to make certain you and Jake meet at his office this afternoon, if it was something he could have told you over the telephone.'

That was correct, and Liz was impressed by Mr Bartlett's perception. That statement also increased her sense of bafflement. By the time she and Mr Bartlett went out to the kitchen where Jake's mother was waiting, Liz felt as though she had a full-fledged mystery on her hands. She looked at her watch twice while showing Mr Bartlett as much of the old house as she felt she had to show him, and kept wishing Jake would come back.

They were ready to leave, finally, in mid-afternoon, to go back to the inn so that the Bartletts could freshen up and perhaps even take a nap if they wished, before supper, when Elizabeth wondered aloud if perhaps Mister Foreman had found something among Rolfe Sumner's papers.

Mr Bartlett was doubtful. 'How long has this thing been dragging on, a week, two weeks? Surely, in that length of time, if there were anything, old Foreman would have come up with it before this. I'll tell you my guess: he's figured some way to see that Hammond gets control. Didn't you say he was Hammond's man?'

Liz didn't remember saying anything like that, and now she wondered all over again. She hadn't believed Mister Foreman could be bought or influenced, yet after listening to Jake's father she had another doubt.

They covered the three miles back to town in good time, and although Liz looked for the Sumner car, she did not find it, which meant that Jake was either still over at Edgerton, or was perhaps on his way back and hadn't arrived yet.

She left the Bartletts at the inn after promising to come for them as soon as Jake returned, and as soon as they could come back. She had no way of knowing when Jake would arrive, but she made a tentative dinner-date with them nonetheless. She wanted to give them a home-cooked meal, but that seemed improbable for tonight because she had no way of knowing how long she and Jake would be over at John

Foreman's house.

As she told her grandfather when she finally got back home, she couldn't remember another day in her life that had been as indefinite, as up in the air, as this day had been — and still was.

It looked better an hour later though, after she'd bathed and changed, and had gone out back to relax, when Jake drove up and came around to where she was, looking a lot more hopeful than he had looked the last time she'd seen him. She let him tell her his news before she recounted what she'd been through. His news was very elemental; he had hired a young attorney who knew the land laws very well, and he had hired him for a low fee. The attorney had been cautiously hopeful. It was true in some circumstances that an adjacent landowner got first and last bid on a piece of ground, but all that meant was that if someone else wanted the same land, they could throw the bidding into public domain, and that way the sale of the land was determined by the highest bidder, exactly as most other land sales were conducted elsewhere.

Liz explained about John Foreman coming out to the farm. She also mentioned what Jake's father had thought. Jake's hopeful look diminished slightly but he did not look defeated. He looked at his wrist and said he was starved, he hadn't eaten since morning, but maybe they should go right over to Foreman's office.

Liz took him firmly in tow, returned to the kitchen, sat him at the kitchen table and proceeded to make a cold-plate, belated luncheon that would tide him over until they met his parents for dinner. Her grandfather, who was doing something out in the toolshed, did not come to the house during the period she and Jake were there in the kitchen. It was just as well, otherwise she would have to explain everything all over again and she didn't feel quite up to that. She did, however, leave a note for her grandfather to clean up and be ready when she and Jake returned for him, because they were all going to the tavern for dinner again tonight.

Out on the front porch Jake waited a moment, while she closed the door, then let out a big sighing breath of air. He didn't say anything, but then he didn't have to because Liz understood that sigh; she felt the same way: whatever was going to happen to them with relation to the Sumner farm, was going to happen this afternoon, and her feeling told her that nothing was going to be able to reverse it if it were bad.

On the way out to the car she noticed that he had had it washed while he'd been up at Edgerton. That was one thing people used to smile about; old Rolfe Sumner never washed his cars.

They drove up through the residential area with shadows forming, long and pale and lean, as the blood-red sun settled closer to the notch in the westernmost mountains it dropped down into these days, and saw boys having a rock-fight across the lower end of Main Street, which they avoided easily, then Liz saw Agatha Thorpe on her way home from the library, and waved. Agatha stopped and waved back, then she turned ever so slowly to watch the progress of the car. Liz smiled to herself.

The village seemed to contain more life in late afternoon than at any other time of day, and for a most excellent reason; until the sun sank lower than the tallest treetops it was just too blessed hot and humid this time of year for most folks to do their shopping. Vermonters, by natural conditioning through long, bitter winters, were not capable of standing a lot of summer-time heat. Fortunately, they did not get too much of it.

They cruised slowly on up to the turn-off for Elm Street as though they hadn't a worry in the world, and as Jake made the turn Liz said, 'I don't know whether it's the suspense or whether it's the hoping, but I'm beginning to feel like a child waiting for her father to come home from work to find out whether she's to get a spanking for being bad, or not.'

Jake smiled understandingly. 'We never should have let ourselves get so involved with the Sumner place. If something goes wrong now we're going to feel badly the rest of our lives.'

He came to the front of the Foreman place, and up ahead was the same unwashed, late-model car that had been parked ahead of them on their previous visit. Bob Hammond had already preceded them to the meeting. Liz did not remember Mister Foreman saying anything about anyone else being present, but it didn't really matter. Hammond was a logical person to also be present.

She leaned, kissed Jake's cheek, and jumped out of the car ahead of him, waited until he came round to her, and smiled at him. 'Buck up,' she said, looping her arm through his arm. 'Even if we are disappointed, we've still got something else.'

He clamped his arm to his side, squeezing her arm as they started up the walkway. 'Win, lose, or draw, I'm still the luckiest man in Vermont.' He paused. 'Come to think of it, that makes me also the luckiest man in Kansas or Nebraska.'

She was thrilled and showed it by blushing. When John Foreman came to admit them to his house, and his office, she looked past and got a surprise; Eulalia Wilson was over there in the office on the opposite side of the room from Bob Hammond. The liquid dark eyes lifted, and when they rested upon Elizabeth one of them dropped in a very deliberate wink, then rose again. It was mystifying, but it was also reassuring.

21

The Unbelievable Moment

Old John Foreman offered his latest guests chairs, then went briskly back behind his desk and scouted through the papers in front of him until he found his glasses, and as he adjusted these to his nose he looked owlishly around and said, 'Well, now that we are all together, I can proceed. There has been a fresh development to the Rolfe Sumner case.' Foreman paused, swung his head slightly and fixed Bob Hammond with his stare. 'A last testament has come to light. It's not the most perfect example I've ever seen, but the law recognises every man's right to make disposition of his effects as he sees fit.'

No one said a word. Elizabeth had always heard that Rolfe Sumner had no

294

living kin. She was intrigued by the fact that one evidently had turned up. At least, that was how she interpreted John Foreman's preliminary remarks. Then he spoke on and she was, for a while, more baffled than ever.

'There are certain specifics people ordinarily follow in the making of a will, but in the eyes of the law any last testament that can be proved valid is acceptable.' Foreman peered at the papers atop his desk, selected one and held it up. 'This paper was witnessed by Mrs Eulalia Wilson a week prior to Mister Sumner's passing. It leaves his entire estate to one Jacob Bartlett, his hired hand.'

For ten seconds it was quiet enough in the little glassed-in office to hear Liz's sudden sharp gasp and nothing else. Bob Hammond straightened in his chair, slowly and truculently. He stared at Foreman for a long time before speaking, then he said, 'Wait a minute, John. How can you prove Rolfe wrote that thing?'

Foreman had an answer ready. 'Because Mrs Wilson witnessed it, Bob. And also because after she brought this to me yesterday. I sent a photostat of it to the County Clerk for the handwriting to be compared with property deeds and tax records at the court house Rolfe Sumner had written out. I got the affirmative confirmation back last night. Rolfe Sumner wrote this will.'

Hammond reached and Foreman handed him the paper. Hammond scowled over it for a long time, then tossed it back and shook his head. 'If that thing's a genuine last will and testament I'll eat my hat. Anyone could have got it up. The signatures aren't even notarised. John, if you try to pass this off as old Sumner's last will I'm going to take you to court over it.'

Foreman was also prepared for this. It seemed that once he had decided his course of action, old John Foreman, the retired big-city lawyer, planned ahead just as he must have done years back when he was matching wits with men a lot more formidable in the field of law than Robert Hammond.

'Bob, you go ahead and do whatever you think has to be done. I'm satisfied this is a valid will. I've taken it up with the superior court judge, and now I'm going to probate it. It's only fair to warn you that unless you can prove falsehood you'll be wasting a lot of good money trying to make something out of this in court.'

Hammond was red in the face. 'John, Mrs Wilson and Bartlett here are friends. It's common knowledge all over town that when he'd visit old Rolfe he'd also stop and visit with her. Does that mean anything to you?'

Before Foreman could answer, the liquid dark eyes of Eulalia Wilson were fixed with an obsidian brilliance upon Bob Hammond. 'Are you trying to say I made up this paper? Is that it, Mister Hammond? You are accusing me of doing something dishonest with Mister Bartlett, is that it?'

Foreman rose behind his desk, and

this time he was in time to prevent trouble, but only because Eulalia had asked questions and was awaiting the answer that did not come.

Foreman's tone was sharp. 'Whatever Mister Hammond is implying he will have his chance to prove in court, not here in my office.' Foreman removed his glasses and put them atop the papers on his desk. 'I told you all I'm perfectly satisfied this paper is genuine. After all, there is something else. I was Rolfe Sumner's attorney for forty years, even when I practised law down in the city. I have a file bulging with examples of his handwriting, not only that but also with his phraseology and his spelling. As I told the judge this morning, if Rolfe Sumner didn't write this will, then it had to be his ghost who did it.' Foreman looked at Bob Hammond. 'Think it over before you do anything rash. Half of this town knows Rolfe Sumner's handwriting, Bob, and they will testify favourably, as will I, if you make a court case out of this. You'll lose, sure as the devil.'

Hammond rose, stiff with anger. 'We'll see who loses,' he growled, and turned to go stalking out of the office. He slammed two doors after himself, the one from the office and one from the house.

Not until the last echo had died did anyone speak. John Foreman sat down again, and wanly shook his head, but there was a tough, hard brilliance to his gaze when he smiled at Jake and Elizabeth. 'Well, that's it. I can't tell you any more. I'll put the will up for probate, and in due course when all claims and so forth have been satisfied, you will own the Sumner farm, Mister Bartlett. As for Bob Hammond's threat, don't take it too seriously. I've known *him* a long while, too. No Hammond ever risked a red cent if he thought the odds were less than sixty-forty. Let Bob think it over a few days. He'll come to his senses.'

That ended the meeting. Jake held the front door for both Liz and Eulalia, shook hands with John Foreman, thanked him, and walked slowly down to where the women were waiting near the kerbing, in the gathering gloom of evening. Eulalia looked up when he came along, then she said, 'It never occurred to me, even when I witnessed his signature on that paper, to pay much attention to it. Not until yesterday when John Foreman came to ask if Rolfe had left any personal effects at my house when he died.'

Eulalia was embarrassed. She wrung her hands and looked anguished. She was one of those people who, by temperament, considered every fight their own, whether it was or not, and this one at least came close.

'Robert Hammond was very upset. Also, he isn't a good man to fight with, even my husband used to say that. But then, if he tries to make me look like a liar or some kind of crook, I'll be justified in fighting with him. And I'll do it, too!'

Jake took both women by the arm

and steered them to the car, put them side-by-side in the back seat, then drove around to the business section of town where Eulalia's house was. There, he kissed her cheek, saw her to the door, and told her not to worry. It was easy to say, but she would worry anyway, and in fact so would he. As he got back into the car Elizabeth came up to ride beside him in the front seat.

'I'm still too stunned to believe it,' she confessed. 'It's so unbelievable. We went over there half-believing we were going to be ruled out, and instead we came away owners of Sumner farm without it costing us a cent. It's too sudden and too surprising.'

Jake drove for a moment in silence, then told her something that was different from what she had just felt, had just said. 'Maybe I should have anticipated something like this. I guess someone with better perception or more confidence would have. Rolfe Sumner and I had several talks about the farm. He told me the last time we discussed crops that I was the first hired man to argue with him about what to plant. He said it showed a feeling for the land he'd always valued in men. There were a few other things; maybe I should have guessed he might name me his heir.'

'You never mentioned any of it,' accused Liz.

'I didn't think much of it,' Jake said, in defence. 'Especially some of the things he said just before he died, at Eulalia's house. You don't take seriously sentimental things a sick person says, Liz. He told me that after he was gone he'd like to think of Sumner farm being in the hands of someone like me who appreciated it.'

Elizabeth rode for a while in solemn thought, remembering Rolfe Sumner. As a child, on the basis of what she had heard, she had feared him very much. A little later, as a young girl, she had viewed Rolfe Sumner as a freak because he did not have a wife, and still later, as a young woman, she had wondered why he had never married, and instead of fearing him, she had pitied him. But never, in her wildest imaginings, had she ever for one moment thought that her future would in any way be related to Rolfe Sumner, the skinflint-bachelor farmer.

She said, 'I was so wrong about him. I think most people were.'

Jake pulled up outside her house and her grandfather appeared on the porch, very presentable with a tie and jacket. He came down to the car looking quizzical and anxious. Liz said nothing until he had climbed in the back, then she told him what had happened at the lawyer's office.

Old Jasper was flabbergasted. He looked from one of them to the other, and finally he muttered, 'I don't believe it. Not old skinflint Rolfe Sumner!'

They drove half-way to the inn to pick up Jake's parents before it soaked in, then all Jasper would say was, 'Sakes alive, I never heard the like of it in seventy years. Never. Sakes alive.'

The inn had a lobby of sorts. It had in historic times been the tavern-end of the inn. Subsequent owners had done their best to make the large, low-ceilinged room resemble a lobby, but there was something about the room that, despite the lack of a bar, the mugs and kegs and bottles, still put a person in mind of a bar-room the moment they entered. In fact, when Jake's parents rose from chairs where they had been sitting relaxed and comfortable, Jake's father said, 'This is the darndest village I was ever in. Across the road and northward a piece is a tavern that *looks* like one, and doesn't serve alcohol in any shape or form, and here at the inn there is a lobby that makes you think of beer and ale, and yet it isn't even a tavern.'

They all laughed and trooped out to the car. It was there, as they were climbing in, that Jake explained to his parents what had happened at John Foreman's office. Both the Bartletts were as stunned as Jasper Carleton had been. Mr Bartlett recovered faster, though.

'What did he give you in writing, son? I'm not doubting Foreman's word, but I just always feel better when I've got something in writing.'

Liz smiled and said, 'In a day or two.'

Jake's mother finally found her voice. 'Gave it to you; that delightful farm north of town. Just *gave* it to you.'

Jasper explained succinctly. 'Ma'm, where old Rolfe was going, he couldn't have sold it and taken the money with him.'

Jake drove slowly up to the far intersection while the others talked, turned and drove back a short distance to a parking spot outside the tavern. There, as he switched the ignition off, he said, 'All out, folks. We can continue the discussion inside. I'm still hungry and I ate before going over to John Foreman's place.'

Liz cocked an arched brow. 'I'm not at all sure I like that. After all, I'm the one who fed you.'

Jake held the door for her, the others were already out and moving towards the doorway of the tavern. Jake leaned and kissed her ear, and reached with a strong arm to encircle her waist, but she sidled clear, turned and scowled. He shrugged it off. 'I want the world to know,' he said. 'I think I'll make a public announcement inside, as we sit down to dinner.'

Liz said, 'I'll kick you in the shin, Jake Bartlett!' and stalked on after the others.

They were early, so they had a pick of tables. Where they sat, finally, was slightly apart from all the other tables, in a candle-lighted corner. On the walls behind them were Currier and Ives prints, and a rack of old pewter mugs that Jake's mother admired for their antiquity, and which his father admired for what they had once held.

When the waitress came they all ordered, and afterwards Jake wondered aloud how long dinner would take. When his father looked quizzical, Jake said he and Elizabeth had to see the minister yet this evening. That drove all the older people into a long, solemn moment of silence, like a requiem. It was Jake's mother who recovered first. She leaned and placed a hand over Liz's hand. 'Welcome to the family. I don't think Jake could have done better if we'd done the selecting for him.'

Jake's father reached out too, his broad, strong hand dropping feather-light atop the hands of the two women. 'Anything you want, any time,' he said, 'just ask. If I'd had a daughter I'd have wanted her to be just like you — independent and just a little tough, at times.'

Liz and her grandfather exchanged a look, but she couldn't see him too well through the floating mist that obscured her vision.

22

A Time of Promise

It would have been nice if they could have had a bottle of champagne with their dinner; this was a kind of celebration, but as it turned out they had to drive back to the Carleton place after eating, and there Jasper rummaged in the kitchen cooler for a bottle of California red wine, a kind of pseudo-champagne, which did very nicely.

They sat in the parlour comfortably talking, and it may not have occurred to the older people, who were lethargic from their meal, who were perfectly content to sit, that the younger couple were restless. The best indication was that Jake sat on the edge of his chair and Elizabeth kept jiggling her foot over beside Jake's mother on the sofa.

A lot was said about Rolfe Sumner, and it was quite different from what most people had said about him when he'd been alive. Jasper recollected virtues that seemed at variance with what old Jasper had said only an hour or two before when he'd heard that Sumner had left the farm to Jake. But Jasper was honest to the extent of saying he had never expected such generosity, and he had known Rolfe Sumner close to seventy years.

This observation inclined Jake's father to reiterate an old axiom about not really knowing people regardless of how much one associated with them. He also speculated about Bob Hammond, but Jasper, like John Foreman, scoffed at a fight.

'Not Bob; he may have been angry at John Foreman's place, but when he's cooled down and thought it over, he won't make a battle out of it. Especially when Foreman said he'd testify along with half the town that Rolfe's last testament was genuine. Bob Hammond didn't get where he is by bucking the odds.'

Mr Bartlett subsided on the Hammond issue, evidently willing to concede that Jasper knew more in this area than he did. It was Jake's mother, still with half her wineglass full when everyone else had emptied theirs, who looked fondly on the younger couple and said, 'Why don't you two run along; dad and I can get back to the inn with no trouble.'

Jasper looked up. 'Sure. I'll drive them back. You two — no sense in sitting around with the oldsters.' He winked.

Elizabeth rose first. All three of the men eyed her with admiration, and although her freshly-done hair and the new dress had something to do with it, there was a lot more to it than just those things. She was a beautifully proportioned woman, and at nineteen — nearly twenty — was at the prime of her youthful beauty. She would be more stunning when she approached forty, but no one could have made her believe any such thing at nineteen; at that age, forty was ancient.

Jake took her wineglass, and his, placed them atop the mantel, turned and smiled at her grandfather and his parents. 'We'll see you all tomorrow. Good night.' He followed Liz out of the parlour, and for as long as they were in the house, not a sound came from back there where the older people sat. It wasn't hard to imagine how the thinking was going back there in the parlour; older people never tired of re-living their own youth, of remembering how it was when they too had longed to get away by themselves on a late-summer warm night.

As they got into the car Jake blew out a big breath, then smiled. 'You'll have to direct me to the preacher's house.'

She agreed, and directed him square by square, but when they arrived over by the white-painted wooden church, another antique even to the hand-made, very uncomfortable pews made of oak and maple, she also told him that she had contacted the minister by telephone and had encountered a pleased welcome to be married in the church any time she wished.

'I said next Wednesday, Jake, but left it subject to your approval.'

He halted in front of the church. It was dark and closed, but the house next door, also painted white, which was the rectory, was cheerfully lighted. He knew the minister only by sight and recalled him as a man of youthful middle-age with a look of health and strength, who had a quick and ready smile. He nodded. 'Next Wednesday suits me — if it can't be any sooner. I'll need a little time to drive back to Edgerton and buy a suitable set of togs.' As the car eased forward he said, 'You could go with me. You'll probably need something, and anyway maybe you'll want to help me decide on the suit.'

She would, of course, need some things, but especially they would need a marriage licence, which could not be had in Washington, but as far as her wedding dress was concerned, she already had it. It had belonged to her mother, and had been treasured in a cedar-chest ever since. Thinking about that made her quiet as they cruised back through the lower end of town. Just before Jake made the turn to cross the steel bridge he paused and squinted over at her. 'Are you feeling all right, Liz?'

She fought clear of the cloying reverie and smiled at him. 'I never felt better. It's just that — every once in a while I feel weepy.' She snuggled over closer on the seat and laid her head on his shoulder as he resumed driving. When they clattered over the bridge she could see out the front windscreen where stars as brilliant as diamond chips were fixed in a dark blue sky. The moon was elsewhere, she could not see that, but on a night like this, contrary to what the writers and romanticists said, she did not need a moon.

They drove without haste to the top

of the bluff, parked off the roadway and left the car, as usual, to walk ahead and see the night-time view. It was a strange night, in some ways. For example, although they could see the village lights and could imagine the houses down there, the people, the unchanging roads and characteristics of this world of theirs, despite the darkness that kept them from being able to see more, each of them could visualise the future as though it too might be visible.

Elizabeth saw herself with small children, saw herself laughing with Jake, saw them both keeping the fabric of their life together sane and sensible. She could imagine him ageing, getting little crow's-feet laughter-wrinkles up around his eyes, his face tanned and weathered, saw him thicker than he now was, and could picture herself a little thicker too, greying, hovering as their noisy brood matured, ever anxious and ever watchful, standing on moon-light summer nights looking out over their farmed fields with Jake, and standing next to the blazing hearth watching her children decorate a Christmas tree in the dead and hush of a bitter Vermont winter.

For Jake, the sights were similar, except that his imagination divided his time between the house and the outbuildings. He broke the reverie for them both by saying, 'We'll raise our own hired hands. That way we'll be sure of summer help.'

She looked over, eyes bright. 'Not always. They'll want to go to Scout camp in the summertime, Jake, and after a while they'll want to own cars and go exploring, go try their wings.'

He grinned, a bit wryly. 'You're pushing them through life pretty darned fast, aren't you? I'm sort of savouring it a year at a time. We'll find a good fishing hole, and we'll go on picnics back at that lake where you and I went. We'll have special pens for their sheep and calves, their chickens and turkeys.'

'The girls too?'

'Sure, the girls too. Didn't you ever want a lamb or a calf all your own?'

She hadn't, but she tempered it for him by saying that living in town, there hadn't been enough room.

He thought dolls were all right, in the house, but outside a girl should learn about animals, about land and people, about towns and mountains, the same as boys should also learn about those things in order to be qualified for life, when the time came.

Liz liked the sound of that, although as a matter of fact her own ideas were less positive. 'Have you thought this out before?' she asked, and watched him nod.

'Yes. But not too long ago. Lying awake out there at the farm gave me lots of time for thinking.' He took one of her hands and held it. 'I suppose everyone wonders how it will be different for their kids than it was for them.'

She thought she understood the thought behind that statement; the

316

thought behind the grim, bleak expression on his face. He confirmed it by speaking again.

'Whatever our kids have to go through, later, I'd like to know we prepared them for it as best we could, and we gave them a heritage of toughness, of resourcefulness, of the kind of tough-minded resiliency people are likely to need a few generations hence.' He stopped talking and turned. 'Does that sound wrong to you?'

She squeezed his fingers and shook her head. 'It sounds right. Washington is an illusion, really. Life isn't like this, most places. But it's an ideal spot to raise our brood. They'll learn to love what's serene, while being prepared for what's different. I hope we can do this for them.'

He slid an arm round her waist. 'It'll be a challenge. I guess we'll have plenty of those to face, too. Together we can do it hands down.' He tugged her closer and the lopsided old moon soared above in its setting of star-clusters.

'We've got a two-thirds head-start on most people our age just starting out.'

'And perhaps instead of naming our first boy Jake or Jasper, we ought to name him Rolfe. It's a nice name — a sturdy New England name. Rolfe Bartlett.'

She got no argument from Jake. 'But the first girl will be Elizabeth.'

She suddenly remembered something she'd been meaning to ask him; she had been introduced to his mother as *Mrs* Bartlett, and although she'd waited patiently to hear his father call his mother by name, Mr Bartlett never did.

'Jake, what is your mother's name?'

'Margaret. Didn't I tell you that?'

'No.' Liz liked the name, it was common and it had a good sound to it. 'Let's name the first girl Margaret Elizabeth.'

He squeezed her, hard, and when she gasped he loosened his grip a little. Behind them a car came toiling up the north side of the hill, topped out, went pantingly across to the southern incline and started down. It wasn't very late at night, but as a rule traffic around Washington diminished right along with daylight. Before the advent of television the bold younger people used to make the long drive up to Edgerton to see a movie, but nowadays it hardly seemed worth the effort, even in summertime when all television had was re-runs of things people had watched last winter.

The sound of that solitary car continued audible even down where it crossed the steel bridge and headed up in the direction of town. 'Someone who went to Edgerton today to do their shopping,' opined Liz. 'Probably stayed over for supper, and are just now getting home.' She chuckled. 'Profligates, abandoned wantons, staying out this late at night!'

Jake laughed. 'Speaking of wantons — I had an idea yesterday. What do you think of a real tavern here in town? A place where folks can go of an evening and have an ale or two.'

She looked around at him. 'You'd

run it?' She was flabbergasted.

'No, I wouldn't run it, but I wondered about starting it, about owning it. It couldn't make much money, but it'd more than pay its way, I think, and the Lord knows Washington could use one. A decent village pub.'

It was such an alien thought to what else they had been discussing, she stood in long silence, but eventually she saw his idea as an investment, and she agreed privately that the village could certainly accommodate a decent pub. Maybe, then, her grandfather and the other men around town would stop making that abominable homebrew, too. She leaned sideways against him and said, 'Do we have to decide right now, tonight, about future investments?'

He tilted her face to find her lips, and in the moment that followed she felt her inhibitions slipping away steadily and totally. Neither of them even remembered what they had been talking about moments before.

Somewhere down across the river in the middle distance a dog barked, then reared back and sounded at the moon. He was probably a raccoon or a bear dog, and this was a night especially adapted for hunting in moonlight. Otherwise, though, the night was hushed and warm, was quietly drowsy, even atop the mustardy coloured old cliff where Jake eased back a fraction and told Liz one more time that he loved her.

Whatever else was in the world, good or bad, tumultuous or silent, was a very long way off; if there were insoluble problems, no one in Washington, Vermont, went to bed troubled by them. In the backwash of life in America as it had been for centuries but was no more, it was still possible for a pair of lovers to stand bathed in starshine and moonglow, confident of their future; confident enough to be willing to take its challenge by bringing their counterparts into a world already surfeited with the counterparts of other lovers, but only confident because where they stood, in the centre of an enduring way of life people had made a point, perhaps inadvertently, but had still made a point, of keeping their world the way they wanted it to be.

It was for Liz, love in her new world, but even so, what she had, what she expected, and what she would get, was the new world superimposed upon the old, and that was a very good kind of a world for her. If change came, it would have to come slowly, would have to allow her time enough to make the transition. As she clung to Jake in the moonlight she was not conscious of this, except perhaps in her secret heart, but eventually she would see how it had to be, but because she had her love, and all he meant to her, she would always be able to accept change.

In fact, when he held her close and seared her with his hungry kisses, the change for Elizabeth was already beginning. As a woman who had found a mate, she would never again be a girl.